T0113779

This Side of Nothingness

A Novel

Mohamed Gibril Sesay

This Side of Nothingness

ISBN: 978-99910-921-7-1

Sierra Leonean Writers Series

&

Karantha Publishers

For Tha Iye

ZULAIKHA'S REVENGE

Mother poked the wind towards man with plump body and dollop lump for head and said to Younger Brother and me, 'if I had had my heart-way, that man would have been my husband.' To which Younger Brother protested, 'I don't want him for a father.' To which mother replied, 'but I would not have given birth to you.'

Eating bitter dreams in an unwashed bowl of memories I contracted cholera, I mean cholera of words vroooo like blood from the slit nape of the woman who would not sing the rebels' refrain: 'we want peace.'

Ah, so you don't know about the rebels' refrain? Okay, Let me tell you: after the Rebels captured our corner of town, they forced people whose relatives they had just killed to sing 'we want peace' to prevent government forces from counter attacking.

'Tell them you want peace,' the rebels ordered. 'We want peace,' the people sang. But this woman refused. 'No,' she thundered, 'we don't want rebel peace.' So the knaves knifed her navel and snapped her nape, blood coming vroo like diarrhea induced by bad food.

So I cussed the cook, a veiled invective. Mother said the worse way to cuss a cook is singing whilst eating. 'How mama?' Younger Brother asked.

Younger Brother always wanted an answer quick quick quick. He was to die because he could not wait, but that story must wait awhile. 'Eee Mama, how, how?' he blurted. 'Just shut off your impudent tunes,' mother yelled.

My fugues are sometimes sweet; they are sugar poured on rotting week-old sauce to make it palatable. Crazy? It happened at Hilltop College, this sugaring of dour soup, at a flat called Harlem, damp as an ill-drained ill ventilated pit- latrine with a leaky roof. There was a professor there, at Hilltop College, his shoes were red-white striped with shoestrings blue, then green socks, pink trousers, brown belt, maroon jacket, green shirt, white necktie, red baseball cap... We called him Prof Rainbow alias Color Rebel also... well, I'll tell you this other name later...

Longtime nor see. How many sleep did you wear during the raining season? Were there holes in your skull, were your dreams leaky, did the rush-rain of events drench your soul with its bloody particulars – slit napes, hammer-smashed balls, upturned labia colored like the under side of a new- babe's lobes? Did you hold your snout when God/ess filled to constipation with our rotten pleas belched for only Hesheit knows how many whatever Hesheit decides to call Hisherit time? God/ess bids Hisherit time like cat a rat. Is God/ess the cat joking with our ratty lives, toss-teasing us about before the final kill? Me? I didn't wear out my sleep; so they have become sleeplessness. My nights are as brand new as this very second. You want some? My nights are for sale – I want someone to give me cash for my insomnia. I go to the university to sell sleeplessness to students studying for their final exams, no need for them to put feet in bowls of water to stay awake, or wrap soaked towels round their famished skins. Let them just buy my sleeplessness made from the finest fabrics of esoterica. But they are so poor, those students. But they wouldn't say that to get my soft-heart to give them the sleeplessness free of charge. Rather they tell me my nights are fake; that my sleeplessness is as old as the squatting buttocks of prophets of yore pouring their thoughts on the deeds of manwoman.

The deeds of manwoman are like hot pap filling up a hungry gut. The gut distends; the fate of the pap is to fill it, to provide a purpose for the gut. But the gut is never glutted. Is God/ess ... remember what we counsel about the dead: 'God/ess has taken himher...' Is God/ess therefore the red-gut where the pap becomes something else? Are prophets the gullets through which the pap pass?

We in this country are pap; even a child gulps us without difficulties. We are pap for the red-guts of flesh- rich gods. We will have trouble carrying these bloody gods to their tombs (but when will that be?). Their corpses will be too heavy. Like the woman we buried last week. So flesh-rich. We called her Balu Bana, which in our language means Balu the big. She was probably created in a night without light, for everything about her was

3

haphazard – great fleshy chunks ill- splattered on ill-shaped bones. Such a waste of flesh was a burden to tote: arms broke, shoulders creaked. But when we gave her to grave I sighed, envying worms of the grave their gravy.

How many sleep did you put on last week? Mine were not beautiful; they were wet rags of nightmare that shamed my soul.   My penis hanged out like a dog's newly separated from his bitch. My nightly bitch had the voice of the orange-selling woman I was licking (which in our area-slang also means 'screwing') but the   body of a   tortoise. I put my thing inside the tortoises' anus. The tortoises' rear hole was hot as baker's fire (you just ask the male agama lizard why its head is so red and he'll tell you about the head's misadventure into tortoise's hot-hole). My penis? It was baked in the succubus' anal fire; it was bread served to hungry electors – that they leave not the party of our flesh-rich gods. That was what they did to the private parts of our neighbor's child; so handsome, this child, like Anabi-Yusufu...

Who is Annabi Yusufu? asked Younger Brother

Eeee, Younger Brother, so you don't know about Anabi-Yusufu... O myth- ignoring youth, I must tell you his story before I continue the story of our neighbor's child. So now listen:

Anabi-Yusufu was the most handsome man ever created, so divine-handsome that he aroused the lust of Zulaikha, his master's wife. She wanted him badly, but Anabi-

4

Yusufu would have none of it. Soon the news of Zulaikha's lust for her husband's slave boy spread and the other ladies of high society started giggling anytime she was around. So Zulaikha planned revenge, a sweet one. She invited the giggling ladies to her house to help her cut onions and other things for a feast... Just when the ladies were slicing the onions she called Anabi-Yusufu. O bewitching handsomeness. O divine beauty. The ladies, lost in the ecstatic apparition sliced their palms for onions without knowing... See the lines on our palms? They are mementoes of the healed-sores of Zulaikha's revenge, mutilations of Anabi Yusufu's supernal beauty.

Rubbish, said Younger Brother, our palm lines are caused by our clenched fist while we were inside the stomachs of our mothers...

Don't argue with me about that, O Younger Brother, I know you are the skeptical type, but listen to this: our palm-lines are caused by that slicing of palms by the giggling friends of Zulaikha; and not by the fetus' clenched fists; no, no, not at all, my dear Younger Brother, they are not marks left by the boxer-like fists of our infant days...

Boxer-like fists? A child was once battered to death by her mad mother because she thought it wanted to give her some upper-cuts with its clenched-fists, 'what do you want to fight me for, me, me your mother, me?' And she rained the most savage of blows on the innocent child...

What did they do to her? Younger Brother asked.

What would they do to a person made mad by our war? They let her go; the war freed her. Like the woman who found herself in the same fleeing places as her son-in law when the renegades attacked her village. Months and months they trekked, woman and son-in –law, strangers in strange places running away from the sounds of war. They clung to each other, intimacy grew and the son in law got the mother in law pregnant. When they finally returned to their village people asked the mother in law, 'what happened?' She replied, 'the war.' And 'the war' became the name of the child. So when the nappies of the child went missing she asked, 'did anyone see the nappies of the war?' So when the child is hungry people say, 'the war is hungry.' The war, the war, the war.

But I must continue the story of our neighbor's child, the one as handsome as Anabi-Yusufu. Its father was a party to its gruesome murder. The father was poor and also bad; so when a politician told him he was paying huge sums for body-parts to make election juju, this bad father gave his son.

This is Ikemefuna in the forests of Sierra Leone. And when the child cried 'father!' this bad father drew his machete and cut the innocent child down, much like Okonkwo did in Achebe's *Things fall Apart*.

Deities, gods, goddesses, in *Things Fall Apart,* the holy text of African literature, there is the story about some deity of Umuofia that demanded human blood. History, fiction and divine myths are replete with man-eating gods. From Aztec to Ur, the gods demanded human sacrifice. But civilization steeped in the myths of the Emperor Constantine has put an end to that.

Who is Emperor Constantine, asked Younger Brother.

So you don't know about Emperor Constantine, O history shallow youth, let me tell you: He was the Roman emperor who converted to Christianity and put the power of the state behind a particular way of looking at the Christ. It is civilization steeped in the assertions of that emperor that put an end to manwoman eating gods in what they now call the West. So now we have god-eating menwomen; god-flesh deifies the masses during mass, what a change of fortunes!

GUTTER FIGHTS AND THE PROUD SERPENTS

Flesh, flesh, flesh, frozen human flesh in the fridge of my bad dream. I don't know who put them there. But I shouldn't let people know they are there. They would say I killed the people and put them there. Salifu is with me in this room that's not really my room but my brother's. What should I do? Throwing the flesh into our compounds' latrine's too risky. Flies buzz the stench of my mulling... Better if we dump the flesh at our neighbors' latrine. No one knows what's going on in my nightmare. My nightmare is as dark and hot as the insides of a pit-latrine. (The shit-heat from the pit-latrine sometimes ripens the bananas of our banana women. They wrap bunches of banana with empty rice-sacks and put them at the far end of the shit-box. And the fecal infra-radiation does the ripening).

But now Salifu is orbiting my confusion like the moon the earth, vexing the waves of my torment. The waves lash against the granite-shoreline of my sanity. The waves of my nightmare are eating away my earth. My earth is a minefield of stories exploding anytime heavy mouths step on it. My mouth has exploded into bloody bits of words staining peoples grey matter (or is it white?) All about these pages you'd be stained with the smuts of my words, like how they say Socrates' words muddied the brains of Athenian youths. The Athenians forced Wiseman Socrates to take hemlock for it. Forced? Well, not exactly, Plato said Wiseman Socrates refused to escape; that Wiseman Socrates said it was impious not to submit to the judgment of the Athenian masses, that for Wiseman Socrates the voice of the masses was the voice of the God/ess, vox populi vox dei.

Shiyor, me nor buy that nonsense, said Younger Brother

Why? I asked.

Younger Brother replied, if the masses' voice were the voice of The-God/ess, then the darkness of their lives would have long become light. Is The- God/ess voice not an irresistible command? Look it up in the books of the Holy Ones: Let there be light and there is light. But how many times have the masses in this man-damn place said let there be light, but get no light as reply. Me nor buy that nonsense, the voice of the masses is not the voice of The- God/ess.

Anyway let me continue the story of Salifu and I in the in the fridge of my nightmare. Salifu and I start carting out the humanflesh from the fridge of my nightmare. Salifu steals a huge chunk of humanflesh from the fridge of my nightmare. Salifu steals it for his soup; long time nor eat meat.

A gutterfight robs me of my tattered sleep. Waking up is undressing oneself of sleep; it's a sort of nudity we sometimes loath. Especially when the reality you wake up to is like Harmattan; and there's no food to warm your soul with. Harmattan   reality! Hmmm, so you don't know about Harmattan reality; it makes your body as white as the insides of a cassava skin, only that your skin is very dry, scaly, and there are no caresses to rub on it. Your skin is evil looking, like chalk-white Bundo girls before they're ritually cleansed. It's ugly; life beats the rib cage of its captivity seeking freedom from your emaciated form. Sometimes you wish the rib cage would give up its reason for existing.

What's the reason for the rib cage's existence? Younger Brother asked.

I answered, the rib cage is the warden of your divine breath.

Anyway let me continue with the story of my waking up to a gutterfight. So I woke up to a gutterfight. Some guys up the gutter hurtled garbage down the gutter. But guys down the gutter pushed it up again. The people upgutter argued, 'why don't you push it furtherdowngutter?' But the guys downgutter howled, 'the dirt is upgutter's.' This annoyed the upgutter chaps and they re-pushed the garbage downgutter to the guys who wouldn't push it furtherdowngutter but upgutter. So they fought there, in the gutter, the dirt flung updown splattering on onlookers and passers-by. Muck on gowns returning from mosque, also called masjid, the place of prostrations, the place of putting your foreheads on the floor and baring your nape to the Lord. 'Here is my nape O Lord, I submit it to your majesty; it is yours to trample upon. I am not even looking, I believe in the lovingness of your foot; my eyes are on the earth, I have faith on the benevolence of your trampling; my forehead on dirt, I reckon you may yet spare my nape the dirt rushing in from the dirt part of my origin.'

'What is the dirt part of our origins,' Younger Brother asked.

I answered, the dirt part of our origins is earth from which we were molded; it is the sperm and ovum from which we were fashioned. Do you like the sight of sperm on the floor, or the monthly flow of ovum on the ground? That, dear Younger Brother is the dirt /side of our origins, the animal part that we must outgrow. That is the dirt of world we want to keep at bay.

The dirt of the world are waves lashing the walls of The-God/ess' house, which as you know, is us; we are temples of the Lord. But the dirt is also us; we rush in with our slime anytime the doors of the temples of the Lord open, staining The-God/ess' carpet beyond purification. The-God/ess every second changes hisherit carpets, only for the new generation to do unto the carpets what others had done unto them, like parents like children. Like Adam like Eve like Cain also called Kabil. Like Set the desert colored one of Ancient Egypt, also called Khmet. Like Sodom like Gomorrah, like Hamana like Judas like Abi Lahab like Abu Jahl like Sir John Hawkins knighted for raiding slaves on the quick-hills of Romeron that is now called Freetown, like Pol Pot like

11

Saybana Sankoh, like Field Marshal Alhaj Reverend Prophet Doctor bla bla bla.

Where do The-God/ess's old carpets go? Younger Brother asked. Are they recycled? Is The-God/ess an environmentalist? Answer me preacher, answer, is The-God/ess a member of the green party?

Somehow, The Preacher replied, The-God/ess' favorite color is green; the people of paradise wear green robes and recline on green couches. Paradise is resplendent with all shades of green.

What about blue? Younger Brother asked. I see blue all over, in the skies, and yonder at sea.

The Preacher replied, those colors are fictitious; go closer, you'll see they are not blue at all.

Younger Brother looked at Preacher with eyes the color of boiling palm-oil and sizzled, 'Close range and afar are different. Reality afar and reality at close range are different. Perception at close range may be fiction to the person farther away. At very close range, everything is dark; the eyes see nothing when something is very close to it. Try it out O Preacher, press something to your eyes and you see nothing.'

The othertime, yea, it was on a Friday, we were inspecting a guard of dishonor mounted by beggars at the entrance of the mosque. Younger Brother looked hard at the festering sore of a mendicant and asked, 'is The-God/ess around?'

And I heard The Preacher say: the genius of The-God/ess is Hisherit ability to make us capable of having illusions that Hisherit is not existing. What! Only manwoman can choose and move towards the non-existence of the divine. Some menwomen are pushed back, flung back to existence by a mystical combination of their volition and the grace of the God/ess. And lo, the light they see momentarily hurts, like in Plato's cave, like the air rushing into the raw lungs of newborn babes.

It's hard at first, the child howls, but breast of mother is chucked into mouth; howling existential hurt silenced by chunks of motherflesh. It cools, hurray for the born again. Not so for the manwoman who has gone totally deaf-blind-dumb as heshe moves deeper into the lie of life without The-God/ess. Death catches himher in unreality; hisher dispositional limbs are amputated, heshe can go no further... So heshe turns round, craving the reality that heshe's unused to... that is hell...

The Preacher went on and on, but I was thinking other things. And this is what I remember of what I was thinking: Is Satan the being still able to crawl towards the illusion of life without The-God/ess even after the amputation of its dispositional limbs? Is that why Satan is nicknamed the serpent? Behold, the serpent is too proud to crave the reality it had mocked and shunned. So it slithers along, smothering the crawling path of those who would ask no God/ess' forgiveness to restore their

13

amputated limbs. It is Judgment day. They know no pleas now would get them their legs. Why then should they give this God/ess the chance to laugh the agony of their penitent souls craving that which this God/ess, anyway, would not give them? Rather Hisherit angels would just remind them (with taunting believers by their sides), you remember when you covet your neighbor's wealth? You remember when you bore false witness? You remember when your worms wriggled in the wrong holes, or when your holes swallowed the wrong worms, you remember when you threw dirt downgutter, you remember when you cooked humanflesh, spewed dirty words on the clean brains of people? When you... No, they would be no crippled rat begging the cat to spare them the agony. They would slither on to the illusion. They would give no God/ess no chance to laugh the greater travails of useless penitence. They would suffer no agony of dysfunctional regret.

But The Preacher also said this about Tawhid, it is the central tent of the faith of the Muslims, that is, those who submit, those who know the peace of existence by truly submitting to the grace of the Creator. Tawhid as a concept, a faith, a belief, relates to, or exposes the unity of being in the sense of all existence being held by the choice or will or grace of Allah…'

How would you translate Allah into English? asked Younger
Brother.

14

'Al' translated into English means 'the' and 'lah' means 'God'; hence a first draft translation is 'the God'. The etymology is also traced to the ancient middle-eastern word of wonderment, lah!!! So it could also mean a being the awareness of who brings wonderment, amazement, awe. It means the being that inspires awesomeness; that makes one exclaim, lah lah lah. And we are told that this Amazement has no gender, neither male, female or neuter.'

The preacher restates his concept of Tawhid, 'Tawhid as a concept, a faith, a belief, relates to, or exposes the unity of being in the sense of all existence being held by the choice or will or grace of Al-lah. There is no ontological division or contradiction between the different epistemological divisions of being. The epistemological divisions are illusions created by our limitations. Fools crave the epistemological illusions; sages and holy menwomen crave the ontological non-contradiction – that is the path to heaven.

Big big English, said Younger Brother, that makes us languish. Nonsense talk hidden in big bigger biggest grammar. For me, Younger Brother continued, the path to heaven passes through the stomach.

Younger Brother sometimes hit the problem on its head. Sure, that was some great philosophizing by The Preacher, but manwoman does not live on theology alone. The morning was dying and I'd still not warmed my Harmattan soul with food... In the freezing

15

Harmattan of the soul, one sometimes wishes hot hell would come and heat you up a little. Our food is hell made small, we eat abused viands - they shouldn't be ours, they belong to the rich manwoman's dogs, the security men at the gates of our dustbin lives. We are walking dustbins that gather the prize-rubbish of the rich... Yesterday Salifu ate off the dustbin of his wife's life.

Salifu is a maggot slithering in the litter can of his wife's endeavors. She totes flies by day and men by night to eat in the morning. The flies are the decorations of her rotten fish business. The fishes are dead rotten before our fishers catch them. Foreign trawlers dynamite the fish-fields of our waters. Their nets also catch the smaller fishes, but they only want the larger ones. So. They cast the dead small fishes unto the oceans of our fishers' exploitation. So. The fishers pass the misery unto the likes of Salifu's woman. So. The fishers' penises are hooks with rotten fish for bait. Lorda mercy, the labia of the likes of Salifu's woman are being caught by the fishers' hook.

Salifu fishes for success with his hook. In the tourist season Salifu walks the tourist beaches nude. Salifu is a beach boy, a handsomely muscular male prostitute with a pus-spitting phallus. I see visions of sick women mistaking the pus for elixir. They are in a queue, orderly, bare buttocks; pubic parts becoming public parts.

What is wrong about that? asked Younger Brother. It is their body, they do with their bodies whatever they want to do with it?

But should they stick them in to my eyes?

Did the sights hurt your eyes? Younger Brother asked. Anyway let me continue with my story about Salifu. Salifu is nauseating. Salifu is the fart of Satan in the crowded rooms of our holy places. Salifu is sometimes me. I'm sometimes Salifu.

THE COLOURS OF SANA'S MOOD

At noon I slithered through the slough of our reality. I wanted to visit Sana the other end of town. But mud upon mud along the way. For long long time now they've been digging brrrrr roads repaired only yesterday; digging out red soil that's red red like kola spat out too soon; dig like rebel-dug highway. Human debris in the ditch digging soil red red like mouth sucking blood; digging machines in hands going rrrrrrrrr like guns in hands of renegades. Our eyes staring at the traffic and the machines, our eyes staring at each other like in a staring contest; our bodies stuck inside taxis and poda poda that are smelling the behind of taxi and poda poda on heat standing still in the palpitating heart of town, blood congealing at letters:

ROAD CLOSED MEN AT WORK

What about women? Younger Brother asked, are women not also at work? This is unjust, very unjust.

Okay, ROAD CLOSED MENWOMEN AT WORK, the arteries of the town clogging like veins of menwomen reading letters of rebels announcing about rebels attacking town tomorrow morning. Digging red red soil redder than sun-party symbol, redder than oil from fruit of frond-party symbol.

When we ask about the digging, this big-man says they are digging for telephone line; that other big man big fool

18

says it is for Bumbuna hydro electric cable rrrr; this other one says they are constructing storm drainages for rainwater and silt from the mountains coming shooooooo in the brrrrrrrrrrrrrshoooooooooorrrrrr, like junta presidential siren speeding through your ears at 8am, 4pm, sometimes even 12 noon or other people-packed hour bringing you to a halt for translucent eyes in translucent jeeps dashing voooooooooooooo in the shoooooooooooooorrrrrrrrrr.

But I survived the rot on the mud. (No boast I'm a practiced mud-walker; an experienced muck-survivor). I reached Sana's leaning house with no mud on me. (O no, Sana's leaning house is not a tourist attraction like that other leaning thing at that Italian place with the edible name. Tourists shouldn't see Sana's architectural miracle; foreign dignitaries shouldn't visit the tilting sides of our spaces and stories. Show them the strong sides – the erect penises, the firm nipples and the beautiful beach-bitchy masks and other carvings masking our ugly existence).

Sana is a manwoman. She-he was born a boy, but a diviner told herhis mother that if she wanted this child to live she should give it a girl's name, and dress it like a girl to fool the spirit of death that had vowed to kill all her male children. Sana's mother had already buried four male children. She was determined to let this new baby live. So she heeded the advice of the diviner and named the baby Sana; and dressed it like a girl; and bought it female toys; and got it to do chores that girls do in

19

this part of the world. Sana was sent to a girls' school. And there it was discovered, just about the time for her-his school certificate exams, that she-he was a boy. They allowed her-him to take the exams, which she-he passed with flying colors. But she-he could not go to university with an F marked on her-his sex column. The spirit of death also discovered that Sana was a man and became very enraged.

But this spirit of death was a child-killer, not a man-woman killer; its enraged blows on Sana's head could not kill Sana. Rather it drove her-him into the outer layers of sanity; she-he became a mad-sane man-woman; the only old boy of the Romeron Secondary School for Girls.

Sana is a poet. She-he loves the path of the pen. In the pen is the pig. Sana is a pig pouring snot on the litter of Romeron. Sana is a rapacious muck-eater; her-his poetry thrives on the dross of Romeron, ordure manures her-his verse. Her-his lines are fresh and green and delicious. They are lettuces, they are cucumbers; they are foreign forms thriving on the feces of our stories. Sana is sometimes me; I'm   sometimes   Sana

Yes, said Sana, *I am the fly who loves the pig's snout. Go ask William Golding, the pig is Lord of the flies? Ask Camus, we are worshippers of the fetish; we go round   the   pig's   head,   we   go around   the   sacrificial   eggs   rotting   at   the   junctions   of   our perambulations. The rotten ones are sacral. We are Jahiliyyans, people of ignorance, people ignored, relegated to the   dustbins   of remembrance; all   the unwanted   in   people's remembrances are thrown at us; we are the replicas of their unwanted Darwinian beginnings – apes; we are replicas of their unwanted divine beginnings – Noah's Ham (Ham is pig made edible, useful. And also laughable, we are Ham actors, we do things badly); we are the spittoons for the phlegm of their souls.*

We raise, nay, lower, our hands as we go around the Kaaba of the time-worshippers of the time-kept city, the ones with three hundred and sixty five gods. This is our supplication: 'here we come, here we come, stuff it into our mouths, rub it on our lips, forgive us our spirituality, bless our buzzing.'

I am the fly buzzing the night soil man' s glove; I am the slime in the line of your vision, the sight your eye shot can not pierce, I am your anti-vision.

I am your poor man. And I am not saying this to get you to get me something. I hate that. Once I cussed a guy who because I said I was hungry wrote a project proposal about giving me remnants of good living. Perhaps it was no remnant, but I cussed him all the same. Not at his face, but in my heart, in the invisibility of my heart. These people just keep lying that they are doing wonderful things towards my stomach. Look, I'm not anybody's cause, nor is my belly, or any part of me. I am a man-woman, not a means to your ends.

I'm poor; dogs lick away my sweat. I don't grumble. Their tongue against my skin is soothing, caressing. One day, I'll lick theirs. I'll bite the dogs that bit me, that's the coming revolution, my revolution. Cry the beloved continent.

Let no one pity me my coming dogness. I am bad. Yes you've had that song. Some Monday for sure, my dogness will show.

Things shall fall apart on that day. I shall no longer be at ease. Not that I'm bound to violence. I'm just a man-woman, an ordinary man-woman, I don't grumble, the tiger does not yell its tigritude. It pounces, some Monday for sure.

I'm the future coiling at some forgotten corner of the present. I'm the midnight child born on the eve of in-to-dependence; the cries o4territorial integrity drown the cries for the integrity of my body. New world order? No, mine is for new body order. I don't grumble. I've learnt to behave like the dog I've become. A dog's dream stays in its belly; a dog's dream can't be communicated. I am a cur fighting bitches in the dustbins of in-dependence. Beware soul brother, uhuru is not yet here. Weep not child, your uneven ribs still have a function. The famished ribs could be used to count. How many ribs have you? One, two, three? Count on thin child, count on African Child, count the bones, the not so good bones, that's the way out of the house of hunger, be the interpreters of our hopes and impediments. I've read a torn copy of that book by Achebe. I salvaged it from the rubbish heap. I read it in the dustbin.

Gabriel Marquez says the end of all good literature is the dustbin. Waw! Garbage cans are minefields of torn knowledge, bits and pieces of classics: Atwood's Robber Bride, Morrison's Beloved, Marquez's One Hundred Years of Solitude, Hawkins' History of Time, Mazrui's Triple Heritage, Carlson's Silent Spring, Cheney-Coker's Last Harmattan of Alusine Dunbar, Patterson's Freedom, Ngugi's Grain of Wheat, Mahfouz' Cairo

Trilogy, Shakespeare's Complete Works, Cervantes' Don Quixote, Khayyam's Quatrains. I was educated by the dustbin, now I'm its chief librarian. My latest books come from the disgraced house of a disgraced minister. He was the intellectual type. When their government was overthrown, the new rulers ransacked his house, looted televisions, doors, windows, everything. But since the new looters were not the intellectual sorts, they threw his disgraced books to the dustbin of my living.

I am an invisible man-woman, but I'm beloved, my tar baby loves me. But because I stink, because I'm the open sore of the continent, she-he also hates me. Should I go tell it on the mountain? Should I announce the dangerous love? Should I feed that story to the famished road? No, I can't grumble; a dog's dream stays within.

It must stay within. I know what happens to those who yell their hell. I know because I had once tasted it. My broadcast of my hurt once earned me a kick, a kick as to the dog of their conception, a kick that hurt me more than the original hurt. I am not grumbling, only thinking, only remembering what happened. Foreign beggars had invaded our streets, they were more efficient. Lorda Mercy, they were taking away the benevolence that was due us the indigenous beggars. So I led a yelling crowd of indigenous beggars to the state house at Fort Thorton.

'Protect your beggars,' we shouted, 'that's the only way they can withstand foreign competition.'

Ours was a legitimate cause, businessmen were demanding the same, the educated were crying for the deportation of milk-teeth

23

expatriates. But no, the riot police was sent at us. I sustained a fractured skull, so now I'm half mad. No, I'm not grumbling, I'm not announcing, I, Sana Tana, am only thinking, only remembering, only dreaming a dog's dream.

I took on the colors of Sana's mood. (I'm a chameleon who takes on the color of the surrounding mood; no better way exists to prey or hide from predators than this. When in Rome do as ... you know the lines). Sana is moody, when I asked her-him about her-his tar baby, his-her mad countenance changed; his-her face became a rainbow announcing hope to her-his flooded soul. The flood of emotions subsided, her-his ark of thoughts rested on his mountainous tongue Ararat, and words – verbs, nouns, prepositions – joyfully trooped out.

Eh man, she-he said, I've laid her, here in this place, she was good, she was sweet; she knows the art

You did it with her in this dustbin

Why are you not using punctuation marks? Younger Brother asked. If you want others to enjoy the penetration of your words you must use punctuation marks.

Ok, dear Younger Brother, in some places I'll use punctuation marks. But let me continue the story about Sana doing it in the dustbin. 'You did it with her in the dustbin?' I asked.

'Yes, and the rats were squeaking in admiration.'

I knew the person she-he was talking about. It was Salifu's wife. So I bragged too, 'I've also wriggled my worm into her hole.'

'Wonderful lines,' he-she said. I'll write a poem about it.'

'That will be good,' I replied. 'But please don't attempt sonnets this time round. And remember 'thou' or 'thee' or 'thy' or putting the verb before the subject is not what makes poetry tick'

'What's poetry?' Younger Brother asked.

'Poetry is writing or saying things in surprising ways that are understandable.'

Rubbish, said Younger Brother. Celestial nonsense... Failing to make sense of the world, poets write handsome nonsense about it. Poets just have this craze for resemblances; they are nothing but rotten creators of warped affinities, making everything resemble every other thing....

Sana looked at Younger Brother the way John stared at an American Professor who reduced arguments into weird figures; they call it symbolic logic. John stared at him like vultures an unattainable rot. The rot is encased in a glass (like laboratory worms). The glass makes the rot expensive. The vultures turn to themselves and say, when has rot become so expensive?

'It's the budget,' says Pote Bra, 'anytime they read budgets prices go up.'

'Well,' ventures Pote Borbor, 'won't they stop reading budgets?

'But it's the exchange rate,' says seller of that smelly condiment called kaynda.

'It's the rate,' concurs the coconut hawker.

'Yes it's the rate,' says the seller of latrine-ripe bananas.

'I'll write a poem about that,' Sana sniggered. 'Folksy Economics' would be its title.'
The other day Sana showed me a short story titled 'Folksy Economics.'

I protested, 'but you said it would be a poem'

Sana replied, 'the story busted the banks of the poem and became a short story. It may yet bust the banks of a short story and become a novella. Anyway let me read it for you:

Chapter One
Bintu, eleven, sat on the edge, drowsing, going down the gutter with all her wares. Not much. Thumb-small polythene wraps of tomato

paste. Not expensive. Those who could not buy the whole tin of tomato paste could afford this. Not much profit. Just about what was needed to get a palm-ful of boiled rice to give the worms of the stomach bits to chew, that they may spare the gut.

Chapter Two
The market keeper, poorly paid, unpaid for months, cane in hand, came along. With the market tickets. These tickets cost more than the profit of the hawkers sweet-singing customers to their wee wares. So those who were not drowsing fled. For the market keeper would seize their wares. Until they paid for the market tickets. But even then, some of their wares would have disappeared in to some holes in the market keepers' office.

Chapter Three
Or the market keeper would just grab their wares and say: this place is prohibited to street trading. Or: your wares are unhygienic. Or: the new rules say ... Or he would just seize the wares without saying a thing.

Chapter Four
So those who were not drowsing fled. Not Bintu. Too hungry, ignorant, tired. Long time since she slept well at night. Floor too damp. Too crowded. Usually slept fetus coiled on one side throughout the night.

Chapter Five
The market keeper prowled. Cane in hand. Towards Bintu. Drowsing. Dreaming: she was in school. Well fed. Her playground was the sky.

Chapter Six
The market keeper's cane went up. High. Higher. Highest. Hurtled down. Untoward. Towards emaciated bones wearing ill-fitting skin...

Chapter Seven
Whaaaaaack! Bintu vaulted, scattering her wares. The market keeper grabbed some. Some fell into the gutter. Bintu gathered what she could and fled. Came again. Behind the market keeper. Daringly. Snatched some of her thumb-small polythene wraps of tomato paste and fled. The market keeper did not chase her. His hands were full with all sorts of wee wares — quarter-parts of onions, clenched-palm small bags of salt. And more. And more.

Chapter Eight
Bintu bowed over the gutter; salvaged some of her wares; wiped off the dirt with a torn end of her tattered clothes.

Chapter Nine
She sat down at the edge of the gutter and started counting the thumb-small wraps of tomato paste. Re-counted. God! She had lost four wraps. Waiii! She dared not go home. She would be flogged. Mercilessly. So she sat there. At the edge of the gutter. Staring at the holes in soles.

There is nothing folksy about this story, I said. And worse, your syntax is un-English.

Sana replied, hail the tectonic syntax shifts that are creating semantic-quakes, tumbling down castles of meanings, freeing slaves tied up by queen-speak.

28

Sana was now agitated. She-he continued, *and the accents became a big flood, rushing against finely built ideas, uprooting meanings, turning upside-down the speech-scapes.*

The English Noahs could not fend off the accents denting the words as they rushed into the new ark called the BBC. So the phonemes became twisted; the squalid condition brought in its wake millions of infections that seized the words by their nether parts. The ark became one of split infinitives, verb-subject disagreements, abused intransitives, disunited tenses and groaning words, filled with the pains of our experiences, singing songs of pain so sweet that others dance to it forgetting the pains

We are masters of Salone English. We are pounding words in the mortar of hope with our pestles of memories, turning them into foo-foo that would go down well with okra-understanding...

I am the Barbarian out here. Some time ago you bounce your language off me to search for echoes of the babbling child that would justify you meting out corporal punishment on my adult self. You bounce your sounds off me to justify the corvee.

I am now a self sustaining echo, now the original sounds of English echo me – I'm bad means I'm good at it, don't dis me man, your children think it's cool.

Sana was now clearly masturbating; her-his mouth was penetrating her-his own ears; she-he was ejaculating happiness all over her-himself. She-he was happy, ah so happy.

Yes, Younger Brother said, Sana writes poems with her-his penis, the pen with the white-ink. That at least does not need foreign exchange. Import substitution, yea, we're self-reliant. When economic sanctions tie me down, I masturbate.

'Yes,' Salifu said, 'to think is to masturbate with the words and vibes you most like or hate. When you masturbate with words you like you feel happy; when you masturbate with words you hate, you feel sad.'

FIRMAMENTS OF OUR LIVES

Salifu's wife, I remember the time I went into
Salifu's wife. AIDS-conscious, I wore condoms.

'Remove those dirty socks,' Salifu's wife shrieked,
'you're entering holy groove; the breath of The-
God/ess is within.'

My rod had become a snake spitting venomous genes.

'Look at what you've done, your semen are now
 stars in my ceiling, you must bring them down before
Salifu comes.'

'Me, bring down my stars?'

'Yes,' she replied, 'your stars are filth in the
 firmament of my life, your stars mock my nights, they
are wicked djinns, they promise all but give nothing.'

'I'm poor, an unpublished poet.'

'You know, I don't lick on credit; I'll publish the
 poem of your disgraceful ejaculation if you don't
hand me your watch.'

'Please don't publish my semen, here take the watch'

I got that watch from a fanatic who thought I was an
ardent worker for his fanaticism. (Remember, I could

31

take the colors of the surrounding mood) It was a Rolex; he gave me it when I succeeded in dragging some boys to his indoctrination. But Salifu is now the proud owner of my watch. He tells me his wife said I pawned the watch to her to get... Well, Salifu says his wife would rather not tell him for what. Salifu is a big-fool-man. Anytime I see my watch on his wrist the color of thombi, I cuss him in my heart. Most times Salifu says to me, 'man, try to pay my woman and get back your watch.'

How I cuss him in my heart, rudely, creatively. I tell you my heart is rude, my heart feels things about people that my mouth is afraid to say. My mouth is my heart's cork. My mouth is a bully, a warden of my imprisoned heart. Freedom fighters free hearts, they pull them out of rib-cages with iron- extensions. Blood upon blood... O resemblances, they keep interfering with my tale. What I really mean is my mouth bullies my heart; my mouth belongs to the oppressor class. One day my heart will overthrow my mouth (sometimes I'm an idealist-communist). I yearn that day when this comprador mouth will be overthrown. But now my heart must make do with tricks (othertimes I'm a rogue-realist). Yes, sometimes my heart fools my mouth into saying things it is ashamed of – like when it told Salifu about what my stars did to the ceiling of his wife's night.

I was drunk; my mouth was too weak to restrain my heart. I demanded my watch from Salifu. I grasped his shirt-front. I was an orb on which everything swirled, but I was an orb that whirled. My world was revolving a thousand miles a nanosecond, and I was spinning two thousand miles a nanosecond. I grabbed the air of my confusion. My confusion was Salifu's wife's knickers-front.

That was not the first day I got drunk. The first day I got drunk I grunted like a speared hog, 'Papa, Papa, Duramani has given me alcohol, Papa, Papa.' I was carried to Papa; he was standing on his prayer mat, thumbs to ears to say the takbir the start of Muslim prayer. I buckled his gown-front and vomited my wine on his holy mat.

I was whacked like I was never whacked before. But that was in the morning, when I was stark sober. Six strongmen stretched me in air. You'd think they were Zanabia- angels stretching Satan before the fury of The-God/ess. First they doused me with pepper-water, the way Onisaweh douses unguents on that masquerading spirit we call Eastern Paddle.

Ah, so you don't know about Eastern Paddle. Come let me tell you: Eastern Paddle comes from the sea-holes of Magazine- Mabella; it is the Eastern seas coming to town, the town becomes flooded; you need a paddle to navigate the nooks and cranny of the jocosity. The jamboree was once banned 'cause revelers sing-cussed a soldier head of state over a million times, but another, a mehaji from the Bambara Town/Magazine-Mabella Axis unbanned it. This other head/foot/buttocks (cross out the inappropriate) of state was the son of an Imam; he

33

damned the kosher-imams of our times and reinstated the eid-ul- adha Masquerade. That son of an imam was no drinker of alcohol, but he re-opened the breweries that got me into that whacking by Papa. (What did you cross out above, head, foot or buttocks?)

Anyway let me continue with what I was saying. First they doused me with pepper-water, the way Onisaweh douses unguents on that masquerading spirit we call Eastern Paddle. Every part of me got it. 'I'll give you hell on earth,' Papa scowled. He raised his Karawas... O, every weal burnt like faggots. It was my first experience of what hell would feel like. Now anytime I hear the word 'hell' I remember that whacking.

Like when The Preacher was telling us about the wings of the angel Gibril; or was it about Malaikatulmawt the Angel of Death. 'The wings on the right have montages of heaven, and these it shows believers when their lives are taken. The feathery anesthetic makes believers' death painless. On the wings on the left, reserved for infidels, are spine-chillers of hell...'

'O O,' I yelled, remembering Papa's peppery whacking to the point of feeling it.

'Don't cry my son,' The Preacher said, waxing vain at seeing the contorting workings of his hell-talk, 'remembering hell makes one stay within the limits of God's commands.

34

'But ah my people, that's the weaker sort of faith, the faith of heshe who is afraid of hell is the faith of a slave; the faith of one who yearns heaven is the faith of a trader, he wants profit; and the faith of one who obeys God because God is God has the faith of a lover, and this my people is the best.'

The Preacher was definitely quoting Asadullah, whose second son, al-Hussein ibn Fatima bint Abu Ibrahim ibn Abdullah ibn Muttalib of Banu Hashim was murdered at Karbala in a murdering that split the middle nation, otherwise known as Islam, also called dinullah, which in English could mean 'Judgment of The God/ess.'

The fanatic was incensed, 'why say The-God/ess? Why bring back memories of al-lat the goddess of the jahiliyyans? Why are you putting together that which had been smashed when habibullah, the beloved of the Deity took Mecca? Why are you associating the divine feminine with the divine He-ness of the deity? Don't you know woman is from a rib, a bent bone, and could never be straightened? Don't you know she is a warped creation and so her suffixes, prefixes and pronouns should not be associated with the divine? The goddess is from a bent mind, she could not be straightened, so she should be smashed as an example for all the crooked to behold.'

But why this misogynistic streak in the way we should name the divine, when as is written the divine is neither male nor female; when as it is written reference to he should also be construed as reference to she. Ah you remember when the women of Yathrib marched onto Abul Ibrahim to ask about whether the prevalence of 'he' in the scriptures meant the absence of 'she.' No way no way, was the reply from the Deity- on-high, the rights and rewards of the believing man should also be construed as the rights and rewards of the believing woman.

Anyway let me continue the story of Salifu and his wife Yeama. Salifu so loved Yeama that he did not believe what I told him about his Yeama on my drunken night. He told me that two days later. My mouth, having regained its oppressor habits, apologized, 'O it's only rum-talk.'

'I know it's rum-talk, my wife couldn't screw you for a watch.'

Anytime Salifu calls Yeama his wife I laugh within. She's not his wife; she's what we call in Romeron taptomi, which in English means one who just stays with me. Salifu himself told me how Yeama came to live with him. She had no good place to lay head to pillow. She slept with her ten brothers-cousins and twelve sisters-aunts and any-two-of-her- three-stepmothers-not-sleeping-with-her-father. They slept on the floor sometimes under-bed of the things-packed parlor of what we call room-en-pala. But Salifu had a whole room to himself. And every night Yeama would come in the guise of a sex maniac to sleep. One night she brought her nightie, 'I

36

don't like to sleep naked.' She left the nightie when she went away in the morning. The next night she came with a towel and extra knickers, 'I'd like to wash off the stench of sex before I leave this place.' She left the towel and extra knickers in Salifu's place when she went away. The other night she came with extra clothes, 'I don't like to wear the clothes I come here with to return home. I'd like to get out of your place neat and clean.' She left the extra clothes when she went away. Then she came with her wares, 'this place is nearer the market than my parent's place.'

Strange that you got your woman because of a sleeping place, I said.

Every generation its strange ways, Salifu replied. In the 60s it was the cleanness of the bandage around your knees. A young school girl would say, 'see how white his bandage is, that is a wonderful guy, think you should give him a chance.' So the guy was given a chance until another with a whiter bandage came along. In our generation it may well be sleeping places. Maybe if another guy comes with a better sleeping place, my wife would leave me.

I asked Salifu 'why do you say Yeama is your wife? You didn't go ask for her hand, or as they say in some places in Salone, her screwing skills. You didn't put dowry for her. She's a taptomi, a taptomi taptomi.'

37

The smug-scum replied, 'it's not how you get a woman that makes you call her your wife. It's what you do together. We do everything together, stay together, sleep together, eat together.'

I was annoyed (you know sometimes I'm a conservative, some modern trends ruffle me). I shrieked in righteous disgust, trying to reduce to absurdity (reductio absurdum we say in Logic) his libertine ideas, 'do you shit together?'

But the philistine retorted, 'yes, sometimes in the fusion of our pleasures, we excrete feces of joy.'

I was not convinced, and I still believe she's a taptomi. So anytime Salifu calls Yeama his wife I laugh within... a wife? Look, a wife is someone you put kola for, dowry. Your people go to her people, they parley with words, pierce themselves with sharp proverbs and the blood of their memories/dreams mix (shut up you medical fanatic, they don't get aids, close up your vocal cavity, I say, you're, like all fanatics, damn too literal). A calabash is brought forward; in it are needles (get off my tale mate, what you see here is metaphorical, I don't mean those slimy syringes you advise drug addicts not to pass unto one another) thread, sweet kola, bitter kola, alligator pepper and money. The calabash (covered by a raffia-fan on top of which is a mat) is wrapped in a shroud white cloth. (Raffia fan, formertimes, mainly came from Mamunta, where a King

38

called Mansa Munta once ruled; but now the raffia places have been taken over by sugar canes from China). The woman takes the calabash and gives it to the eldest male of the family. They ask her if they should chew the kola and eat the money. If she says yes (she almost always says yes) the marriage is sealed. She's advised, prayers are said, and they carry her to the bed of her husband. If she's a virgin there'll be blood on the white cloth and her mother will keep it as a relic. But that is rare now. If you want a virgin you go to the remotest village in the thickest part of the remotest forest.

Like what Duramani did. But that girl was very timid about sex. She would holler and fight anytime cousin Duramani touched her skirt. We called the girl's uncle, and together six strong men held her tight for brother Duramani to consummate the marriage. Blood spewed on my prying eyes.

Me? I was not a husband. I lacked the guts to shackle a woman or women into my every plan. But when I was in the mood, I had sex-mates. It was easy. A teen-woman toting a tray of oranges or mangoes or shit-ripe bananas would be passing by and you called out, 'I want mango, how much?'

She tells me'

'Sit down, peel one for me.'

She starts peeling.

'Your mango is sweet o, are you sweeter?'

The simpleton smiles.

'Spend some time with me.'

'I have to finish selling this.'

'How much does everything cost?'

'Three thousand leones.'

'O.k I'll buy everything.'

That's it, you have mangoes, you have a girl to, as we say, clean. You become her customer. She comes again and again, and again until you get tired with eating mangoes; so now you go for oranges, 'How much do your oranges cost?'

Salifu thinks he has a better strategy (he lives in a westerly slum and you know the West, even in rottenness, thinks they are better organized); he has provisions: milk, ovaltine, sugar, butter, jam. He shouts out, 'hey you, why not come for breakfast or lunch?' The woman comes, eats the provisions and Salifu's penis too.

It's mutual, the girls are food-starved; boys are sex-starved. So we help ourselves out, it's sweet, it's fine.

The othertime a battered mother announces to her tattered daughters, 'today I have nothing; everyone fends for herself.' So they fend for themselves, and we help them do it. It's sweet; it's fine. Sometimes if we don't have enough money. So. We band together, four five six youths; the money now means something to the girl's stomach. So four five six youths take turns. It's sweet; it's fine. We call it communism, no body's monopoly, equal distribution, we communist the girl. It's sweet; it's fine.

Otherdays it's the girls that communist you. Two sisters and their cousin come. They strip, you strip. You have a good time. They go away, filled with your food and semen. Othertimes it's only your semen and your words. You promise them the next day will be finer. They trust your sex-credit- worthiness. They come the next day for the promise; you give them words and semen. They come the other day; you give them words and semen. They get tired. You look for some others to give your empty words and potent semen. The girls get pregnant; they come with their parents in the middle of a bright day to ask whether you are responsible. You strike a match in the middle of that bright day as if to make the girl see you better, 'look at my face properly, do I in anyway resemble the man who licked you?' The girl becomes a laughing stock; her parents throw her out. Heavy with child she goes from place to place seeking sleeping place and gives birth in between houses.

But you know; I was plentytimes a remorseful actor in the drama of our lives. So I was somehow preachy to cousin Duramani a teacher, a fervent practitioner of the lying game.

'It's ungodly cleaning women on empty words,' I said.

Duramani yelled, 'let priests in fiery sermons melt and wide arch of ranged religions fall, our dying must go on, sweetly; we're sick people consoling ourselves with the little sweetnesses in our dying forms. Dying is an old as living; leaving the world is the same as living it.'

'But you were not like this before; you were a good Christian; what would the priests who taught you say now?'

'And you were such a good Muslim, carrying your father's book to the mosque... To heaven, mate, I'm matured, have kicked my remorse for not growing in to what The-God/ess wants us to be, an image of Himheritself on earth. Impossible! Was Satan not damned for wanting to be the ultimate image of The-God/ess, for representing himself as an equal unto The-God/ess, for making Adamhawa, also called AdamEve, think the same? ...that they would be like The-God/ess? Boy O girl, the world is too small for even two The- God/esslike beings let alone six billion divine...'

My brain dropped down my rectum, mixing with all the incomprehensible filth down there, and I wagged my head at Duramani, 'I don't understand.'

'To be The-God/esslike is to be infinite. But this world is a finite place. The-God/ess puts this idea in us that we are or could be an image of Himheritself on earth to agonize us with its impossibility. So. We're sick, but we think the sickness is caused by our not trying enough. So. We're full of remorse, always on our knees begging for Hisherit mercy... No, mate, I'm through with this game of rats apologizing before the cat for being rats. I was created with a sore, cancer in the genes, entropy, nothing will heal it - neither prayer nor sex nor anything; all we do is without effect. Why then should I spend my dying gazing at its ugliness? No no no...'

'Why then do you fear AIDS, why do you use condoms?'

'Smug-scum, it's not to barricade myself against dying; it's instinctual, perhaps it's only to immerse myself in the sweet fantasy of living, ever living - was I not created with the impulse for life? I have no remorse about using condoms.'

'But you'll die anyway.'

'Sure, I'm a terminal patient taking dope. Everybody has his way; Jesus would not take the intoxicant given to him on his way to his cross ... he was strong enough to face death sane, wearing a diadem of mutilation. My religion says he is The-God/ess, and that Hisherit death was a sort of suffering repentance. Repentance for what? Let me tell you, it is for the suffering hesheit-as-The-God/ess wrought on manwoman; repentance for peoplekind agonizing in the gasping surreality of what Hesheit dreamt into mere clay. The death of The-God/ess is a sort of remorseful act to free us from our remorse. I don't think I like Nietzsche, but I like this message of his. Look mate, don't you see the resurrection of The-God/ess's absence in me, the ascension of nothingness... O mate let me be let me be.'

Cousin Duramani infected me with a craze for neologisms- heshe, manwoman, and most interestingly, The-God/ess.

'Makes you give a better picture,' he said. 'You see, all renditions are inexactitudes, but some are better than others.'

'Why?' Younger Brother asked

'Because Y has a long tail. Just like sperm speeding up the fallopian tube, just like the Y chromosome that is in a hurry to get to the ovum before the X chromosome'

You see, Duramani is mischievous; now he's asking me about   the supply of condoms he gave me.

'Finished,' I reply.

'Why don't you get some?'

'I've been discouraged.'

'By who or what?'

'By Yeama, Salifu's wife.'

'That's why you always have gonorrhea- little ants biting off bits of your penis hole, and when you piss it's like pepper on micro-sores. Tell me mate, how do you stand all that pain?'

'I no longer have gonorrhea.'

'How come mate?'

'Private solution,' I replied.

'Come on mate, I know you're talking about your privates, but what's the solution?'

'Pissing after sex... the soonest I climb down a woman I'm on to the chamber pot pissing.'

'Hmmm!' Younger Brother exclaimed, 'you also believe in that myth?'

'Anyway,' said Duramani, 'how do the women take it?'

'I think they don't like it and I hate it... O how I hate my after-sex feelings.'

'You're making your ugliness worse.'   Duramani replied, 'he who looks back on what he considers improper behavior is like Lot's wife - a being of sourness; a figure of saltiness. You feel the faggots, hell, it contorts your essence, and you pray to The-God/ess to cool your hell. No, do like Lot, he didn't look back: having lost his wife to salty remorse he drunkenly made love even unto his own daughters... that was a beautiful dying....'

When I told Sana about this, he promised to write a poem about it - 'Story *of My Dying*' would be its title.
 The Story of my dying started thirty years ago... I ate my first morsel of touch from a grandmotherly midwife upcountry, at my mother's home village. It was under a coffee tree, beside which they buried my umbilical cord. Now anytime I drink coffee I remember my umbilical cord, and my birth, and my babyhood (as told by my mother).

Were there no nurses during his birth? Younger Brother asked. Is it not very dangerous to be delivered by untrained grandmothers cutting umbilical cords with crude knives?

There was a nurse, Mother said, but she ran away just before your brother's birth.

Why? Younger Brother asked

She misplaced the afterbirth of the chief's wife.

An afterbirth is a birth thrash that should be disposed of, Younger Brother said.

It belonged to the woman who gave birth, so she should dispose of it. Mother said. So the chief's wife bellowed, 'where is my afterbirth?'

'Where is her afterbirth,' the assembled crowd echoed.

The nurse could not produce the afterbirth.

'I have buried it,' she answered.

'Who gave you the permission to bury the afterbirth of the chief's wife?'

I was with the nurse then, feeling the pangs of labor; I shouted at the crowd, the nurse is delivering me now, stay out.

Okay we will wait until she has delivered you.

I opened the backdoor to our house, behind which were coffee trees, and led the nurse through the coffee trees to

47

freedom. But I could not make it to the house. I lay down there, near a coffee tree. An elderly woman saw me and delivered me. I gave birth to you near a coffee tree, and near it I buried my afterbirth and your umbilical cord.

Mother said I was so thin, like a broomstick, so they nicknamed me Sintali, which in our language means broomstick.

And Mother also said; you were always shitting, perpetual diarrhea, so much so that I didn't put any cloth on your flabby waist...

'Ah mama, don't say.' I pleaded.

I'm jittery anytime mother talks like this before my friends. I think they would judge my manhood from my babyhood... I know that's a fallacy, what we call genetic fallacy in logic; i.e. things aren't their origins. But manwoman is not ruled by reason alone... In fact I have a soak (we also call sex-mates 'soak') who always teases my flabby waist.

I protest, 'but you know by the way I go into you that my waist is rock-strong.'

'You're a fool,' she replies,' 'your flabby waist is the source of your sexual prowess, the way you wriggle your backside is just fine.'

And mother also said; your head was so big; your broomstick body couldn't support it; people used to say; this head does not belong to this body. Your head was the laugh of the family talk. Every funny talk ended on your head. 'This is like Sintali's head' was the way to say something was really funny. One day your father cupped your scalp and said to the assembled laughter, this head shall be a great head full of learning... then he caressed it, prayerfully. Everyday he would do this, everyday.

And mother also said; so it was son, you were always crying, as natural a thing as a cat eating a rat would send you rolling on your tears... How we used to beat you for being so rotten- banana-hearted.

'Mama, don't compare me to a rotten banana.'

'Okay, there are no rotten bananas, only overripe ones.'

'They are all the same,' Younger Brother butted in, 'rotten, overripe, too much shit heat on them.'

'Don't mind him,' mother said, 'even such bananas have uses, just mix them with rice flour, put in a pot, get fire under and on top of the pot, and waw, you will have a delicious banana bread.'

Younger Brother asked, 'is it that you can only be useful by going through fire? No, spare me that type of usefulness.'

49

And mother also said; and you were so proud, if your father beat you and then gave you money or some other thing to get you to get over it, you would refuse. You never allowed your weal to heal, you hardly forget. Your father once said, this child inability to forget shall make him be a great tale-teller, but it shall be his undoing, his memory shall one day break his fragile heart...'

And mother told us the story of spider the storyteller.

Spider calls neighbors, 'ah come let me tell you about my mother in law!' The neighbors, itching for news, form a circle around spider. Spider points at his mother in law's compound, 'that my mother in law wets bed!'

'Aaaaay!' the neighbors exclaimed.

'Vomits on herself!'

'Eeeeeee!'

'Shits on herself!'

'Hmmmmm!'

'But the other things, I will not say here, people are too fast- mouthed, they may spill my words to my mother in law.'

'Say!'

'No, except at the sacred grove.'

So they went, leaving behind the uninitiated, those whose mouths had no covers. They went, fast, through thick and slippery, to the sacred grove — any word said there stayed there. They were almost there. Spider turned toward the assembled story-listeners and said, 'we need not go in, I will tell you now... my mother in law spits.'

'What!'

'Spittle, my mother in law spits once in a while.

The story listeners beat him up for wasting their time

And mother solemnly warned me after narrating the spider's tale, 'if it comes to pass that you become a tale teller, don't waste people time high openings and flat endings.'

THIS SIDE OF NOTHIGNESS

The story of my dying is one of a broom wearing out. So now it is only used to sweep the latrine floor. It is always wet with piss - the tears of our dying cells. So now this broom sleeps outside; no thief is so low as to steal a latrine broom.

The nights of my childhood were nights of profuse bedwetting, sorry, mat-wetting, for I was banished from the bed to a mat on the bare floor. The soonest I was off to mat I would piss in the gutters of my dreams. Sometimes it was not a gutter, but a wall or football field. Othertimes I would just wake in a puddle of piss without knowing how I got there. Mother did everything to stop me drowning in the pissy lakes of my night. She stopped me from eating or drinking at night; I mat-wet like I never did before. She woke me up every hour; I mat-wet every thirty minutes. She gave me some medicines that looked like dried cow dung; that only made my piss smell like goat turds. She flogged me every morning; my penis cried every night.

One harmattan morning, my transformation of mother's place into a piss-yard so maddened her that she called my peers, gave them canes, stripped me naked and ordered the assembled barbarity to beat me singing, 'pisabedi!'

I answered, 'jankoliko.' 'Pissabedi.' 'Jankoliko.'

They called me komra, which in our language means suckling-mother; for I was that, always dabbling with piss, always laundering pissy clothes, always hanging clothes and mats under sun.

The sun of my dying behaved erratically. One day it rose in the west and set in the south, giving my east turning leaves a hard time getting its finer energy. The other day it didn't shine at all; perhaps the equally erratic orbiting of my moons blocked its rays.

My moons are my emotions, mostly love for my country. It is an unrequited love. My country goes on oblivious of my existence. Am I not a good enough lover?

My country is a bitch making love to Ishmaelite penises. (I think my outburst is the irrational jealousy of a mad-lover, no problem I'll go on, life's not only about rationalities)   My country is bitchy, it's not even prostitution, the prostitute also   called commercial sex worker asks for money, maybe to feed the family. But my country is a real bitch, literally; the bitch asks for nothing from her curs. I tell you mate, no lie, curs are lucky; they aren't required to take care of their mangy- offspring. (I think I am ranting like a frustrated lover, no problem, ranting is also part of the way manwoman communicates) My country is a masochist, it likes to be gang- raped for the pain of it, it has all the venereal diseases of all the races and mix races of the world- Semites, Kushite and Bastardites; Mongols, Maronites and Maroonites; Anglo- Saxons, Dravidians and Slavs. Yet still I love my country, with all its STDs; yet still it snubs my caresses.

Am I not good enough? I sulk in the night of my noon - at thirty I'm a cockroach eating the bitter pages of my country's sad stories; a roach entering a palm oil bottle; a cow begging the one who sharpens knife to discount the butcher... Tell me which country would love a skunk like this?

But no, on the third day my sun was cold, so much so that the piss-wet mementoes of my nights wouldn't dry up. I shivered like Anabi-Brima in the belly of Namrud's fire.

What is Namrud's fire? Younger Brother asked.

Eee, so you don't know about Namrud's fire, okay let me tell you: Anabi Brima, when Namrud's people were not around, went into their temple and broke down all their god/esses; save the biggest, on whose shoulder he hung the axe. When the people returned and were asking for the destroyer of their god/esses, Anabi-Brima, also called Abram of Ur advised them, why not ask that one on whose shoulder there is an axe? The people replied, but you know they don't talk? Anabi Brima also called Abul-anbiya answered, why then do you worship them? This angered the people of Namrud also called Nimrod, for now they knew Anabi-

Brima was the culprit. They lit a fire so huge that it killed twenty men and scotched the pubic clouds of heaven. Then they flung Anabi Brima into it.

But The-God/ess said to the Angel Gibril also Gabriel, name sake of Marquez the Macondian, Gibril, if that fire scotches a little hair of my friend Anabi Brima I'll punish you more that I'll punish Satan the Serpent also called Iblisa al-Garur, which in English means Iblis the arch-deceiver. Angel Gibril hurtled down the skies like Salman Rushdie's Gibreel Farishta and made the belly of Namrud's fire so cold that Anabi Brima, Khalilullah, which in English means friend of The-God/ess, shivered inside it.

That was how I shivered that morn of my enuresis. Mother, ah mother's love, she felt so sorry for me that she changed my clothes and put me to sleep in bed near her. I pissed on her like I never did before, all part of her. She didn't beat me. One stupid elder around said it was because she might have felt somehow guilty. The piss of a son capable of an erection must not touch the groins of his mother. It's like having sex with her - incest. But perhaps the motive for not broadcasting my piss was not that selfish shame covering. I was then in secondary school, form two, and she might not have wanted my school pals to know about it, to taunt my nights the way to school, in school and from school.

Not so my Younger Brother. He would threaten me with public broadcast of my enuresis anytime I pushed toward hurting his feelings. It was his weapon. He rarely did broadcast, but the threat was there – pisabedi. Just an eye, just a peculiar wink. I was well behaved towards my Younger Brother. But later, much later, he too stopped showing my piss-wet knickers to the inquisitive public. That was because of some selfish thing. I was in form four. But now he too had something he didn't want me to get out to the public. It was a peculiar habit, thrusting his index finger into privates of sleeping girls and smelling it. He liked it. I hated it. But my piss, my mat-wetting. So we had our own version of MAD - Mutually Assured Disgrace.

Oh me, why should I read selfishness into people's motive- perhaps mother stopped broadcasting my mat-wetting because she selfishly wanted to cover a superstition induced incest guilt. My brother didn't holler mat-wetting because of his selfish fears. O me O me, why shouldn't I believe that menwomen could act selflessly... O me O me... O flabby waist rotten-banana-hearted shit-gazing un-Samaritan porter of frozen humanflesh... O idealist-communist rogue-realist remorseful cleaner of soaks... O roach entering the palm oil bottle of his damnation... O moody being... O elder brother of a Younger Brother who loved the fast lane of dying, the dangerous side of life.

Like sniffing the exhaust fumes of vehicles. Younger Brother would chase vehicles lowering his snout to inhale the fumes. He said he loved it; the smell was intoxicating. One day a driver saw him behind his car sniffing the

56

fumes like a cur a bitch on heat. The driver sped on, a little faster, Younger Brother moved on, faster. Suddenly the car stopped. Younger Brother's face bumped into car's iron arse. Blood upon blood. They gave him twelve stitches at the hospital, pain upon pain.

The othertime he bet he would jump from the corridor of our two-storey house to the roof of the next house. Before we could restrain him he was in the air, towards the rusty corrugated iron roof. Feet pierced roof like needle a cloth; a nail struck his scrotum. He didn't cry, but I, with a penchant for imagining pain to actually feeling it writhed in agony. I held my balls hollering like a virgin in labor, her hymen must be torn from within; child deflowering mother.

'Shut up you pig-child,' Papa thundered, hitting my jowl with the back of his palm.

My memories are boats plying the rivers of my insides. Sometimes the river is calm, so calm that the passengers in the boats have a jelly good time; they smile to each other, smile as big as laugh, molars showing. Othertimes the river is angry, there is a Jonah-like tempest and the shadowy passengers in the boat would cry to me, their creator, 'ah absolve us of this ugliness... We don't want to drown in the waters of your fury.' And the Jonah amongst them, the target of my fury, would be cast unto the sea. Today the Jonah is Papa, he's cast unto the waters for flogging me like Mushrik Ummayya the

Qureishi did to Mummin Bilal the Ethiop because I peeped at a bathing relative.

Ah so you don't know about Bilal the Ethiop. He was amongst the first to believe in the message of Abu Ibrahim. But his master, Ummayya would have none of it. Ummayya placed a huge boulder on his chest to force him to stop believing. Bilal only answered, One, One, One.

What! Can't he count? A passerby interloped. Can't he just say two, then three, four...

Be careful how interlope into counting affairs. There was this mad man near a bridge saying repeatedly, thirty-one, thirty-one, thirty-one. A woman going to the market heard him saying thirty-one. On returning from the market she still heard the man saying thirty one, thirty - one.

Don't you know how to count? the woman asked. After thirty-one, we have...

The mad man grabbed the woman by the ankles and flung her over the bridge, thirty-two, thirty-two, he said. He kept on saying that until he got another interloper over the bridge, thirty –three, thirty –three; then another person, thirty-four ...

Anyway let me continue with the story of Bilal. He kept on saying one one one, because he believed in only one

The- God/ess. He would go no further, for that would mean going up to three hundred and sixty five, for that was the number of god/esses that the people of Ummayya believed in

Anyway let me continue the story about my being flogged like Bilal was flogged. Santigie the son of my maternal cousin's half brother's maternal aunt's sister-in-law's uncle, and Younger Brother, peeped at something and called me, 'Momodu come see.'

O it was Santigie's mother's buttocks rotund like well- molded foofoo balls. I only peeped that once, but Santigie and Younger Brother peeped until they were caught. They called me an accomplice. My protest was as weak as the house of spider in a storm of flying pestles. (Though, of course, the house of spider was strong enough to hold back the strength of the giant horsemen of Jahiliyya from harming al-Amin and Bakr Siddique the trembling one, also known as the companion of the cave, whose greatest deed was ensuring the freedom of Bilal the Muezzin from his master Ummayya. Fear not, said al-Amin unto this companion of the cave, The Deity is with us)

But The Deity was not on my side that day, even though I was also on the side of truth. I was caned the greatest for being the older boy who ought to know better. How could I forget that beating; the scars are still here, all about my thirtyish back. One day, a soak-mate asked me, 'ah dear, why all these marks on your skin, were you a thief?'

Thief? Do you know how we treat thieves here? Let me quote you an ill-fashioned poem Sana wrote after seeing what we did to a thief our end of town:

Cables crude
Cut weal rude
Every nook of dude
In unfair feud
Soles flayed
As dude for mercy prayed
O what a kick
On his strangled dick
Stripped nude,
Head shaved rude
Multitudes crude,
In sadist feud
Pierced needle in lime
Pushed thru anal slime
 O inclement social clime

Me a thief? Cane marks making me look like a thief? I was furious, I drowned papa in the waters of my fiery for this. I let them cast him out of the boat. I made him plead, 'cast me out, I wronged my boy.' The waters filled his words, choked his voice, his eyes stared at the watery expanse like one who has unexpectedly lost a court ruling. Then my anger subsided. I let a whale swallow him. For in spite of the beatings here and there he was a very faithful servant to my kingly head.

He paid my fees, bought uniforms, textbooks and when I got good mark at school (which was everytime) he would buy me anything I wanted-footballs, fashionable clothes, shoes.

I was always a king when results were out (true this is not mere boasting; I mean I'm not the proverbial teacher who always tells his student about his own excellent marks at school. No. If you care, check, I really get excellent marks, and Papa would buy me things that would make me glow). So for this I let the whale spat papa out unto the shores of my Nineveh, 'be good son,' he said unto me, 'fear none but The Deity, worship none but The Deity, don't take your passion for a deity beside your creator.'

But cousin Duramani scoffed, 'so this is why you're so remorseful, 'cause you feel you're letting down your good father anytime you lick a girl... I pity you mate ... you know you can't become The-God/ess' image on earth but you act to become it... I know it's a mirage, so I don't make the ritual motions towards it. There's no water there, so I don't loll out my dry grief for a drop that would never come... But you, you're always ranting at those like me who don't give a damn... Come on mate, fowls croak frogs chirp crickets crow, come come dear you need not fear, this is our world the sounds are not strange, cats bleat when thunder flashes goats caterwaul as lightening

61

roars humans bark dogs talk, come come mate do not cry the sounds are familiar...'

But I was crying bitterly, emptying my heavens to water the give-a-damn shrubs of my Amazon world – so damp, so eerie, these under-twines, a thousand scorpions sting your guts.

'Stop crying,' Duramani mock-shouted, 'rotten-banana-heart, your tears are but rills in the wasteland of existence, waters lolling in the dunes of desert-times.'

'What then should I do, cousin, what then should I do?'

'Be happy, soar like a bird, follow the instinctual, the call of your DNA, that's the only way to migrate to the blissful natal springs of nothingness...'

Duramani's words were as tempting as mid-afternoon ablution-water in the mouth of a fasting man. But I held my gullet down; I would not swallow his temptation.

'Duramani, 'I called, 'I was not put on this earth to follow my instincts...'
'I'm not against that,' he replied, 'what I hate is to be sad because you naturally like worshipping your phallus... It's the remorse that I loathe.'

Duramani is irresistible, I know he's a shaitan, a devil, one of those who, as the kitabul huda, the book of guidance says, assail manwoman from behind, on the side, front, up-sky, below ground, but he's just irresistible.

Now he's saying, 'it's all wasted effort, sweeping dirt against the wind, building sky-scraping sand-castles on the shores of the great seas of nothingness.'

'Life,' I fired, 'is a heroic stance against nothingness.'

'But everything is against life; the world moves towards entropy. It's easier to be dirty than to be clean. Just fold your hands and feet and you become dirt, just like that. But to be clean, to suspend being dust, you'd have to buy soap, get water, undress etcetera, etcetera, etcetera. But it's all for naught, the atmosphere dirties you; your own spittle against your skin is putrid, smelly urea in your sweat-holes. We are walking dirt. And both exertions and non-exertions against dirt lead to naught but nothingness. You've ever heard about the tragedy of the bath.'

'No.'

'The man washes off the dirt of his being. But the dirt does not go away. He washes and washes, eroding himself in the process. He washes and washes and washes until his entire being wastes into nothingness.'

63

'Duramani, your groundnuts tempt the squirrel in me.'

'Well then, stop the squirrel in you with the dog in you.'

'Duramani, you are abusing me.'

'The dog is man's best friend; is it an abuse to call you by your best friend's name.'

'Who told you our culture sees the dog as man's best friend,' Younger Brother said. 'You will get into trouble by using metaphors that people here can't relate with.'

'Duramani,' I called, 'is it true that you have FDS, Friendship Deficiency Syndrome?'

'Yes.'

'How?'

'I once befriended without heart-condoms and got infected with the virus.'

'Who was the loved one?'

'My world, she too had loved without condoms, sustaining all types of organisms. But the worm, the same that infected the ears of Eve and Adam infected her... so now my world is unfeeling – and she has a right to, a God/ess damn right to want to marry you to its cold

64

dark unfeeling bowels... Dust to dust, filth yearns filth, what else? From it, creation; unto it death; from it again, wow, resurrection. My earth craves your dying; corpses enrich it.

Duramani's words are flies buzzing my pus filled ears. My ears are rotten, and always itchy – only matchstick, that harbinger of fire, which in the world promised is called hell, could assuage their uncommon itch. I'm responsible for the pus in my ears; the matchsticks irritate the delicate inner-ear linings.

'Yes' Duramani would say, 'the purpose of my words is to buzz the pus that would one day take over your whole being – the grave awaits your total pus.'

'Duramani, the way you talk, you should have become a priest.'

'I was brought up by priests to become a priest. But I got bored, simply got bored by their repetitious rituals. Do you like to eat pumpkin sauce everyday? Variety mate, that's where the pleasure is... today cassava leaves sauce, tomorrow potato leaves, next tomorrow krain-krain, like that like that; but look mate, you must wear condoms, some sauce give aids.'

Duramani is a trickster. He begins his arguments convincingly, and then he veers off a side-meaning of a word to an unexpected destination. 'I got bored, simply got bored by their repetitious rituals – do you like to eat pumpkin sauce everyday? Variety mate...today cassava leaves sauce.' The word 'sauce' is where he changes direction. 'Sauce' in our area-slang also means 'woman' – different sauce, different women, 'but you must use condoms...'

So you see, his rebellion against rituals ends up in womanizing, changing women like clothes you wear – variety.

The Preacher once said, '...the word the word, the different meanings of the word, that's the source of unfaith. Those who have faith follow the established meaning of words; those without follow the metaphorical implications. That's the trump card of Iblisa al-Garur also called Satan, which is very similar to the Ancient Egyptian's Set, the name of the desert one, the infertile one, the evil one who tried to prevent the resurrection of Osiris by the Virgin Goddess Isis. That is his trump card, this Iblisa al garur, he makes you imagine the thousands of metaphorical implication of every word; you now have variety, as the situation predisposes you jump from one meaning to another, you become untrustworthy, skeptical, without faith in anything, you become a heckler, a munafiq, an unbeliever. Is it for naught that the Kitabul-huda, the book of guidance, also called the Koran-ul- Karim, which in English means the Respected Recitations, curses those who follow their imagination!

'The battle now is in the realm of the word; Must it be licentious? Remember the Jihad of Uhud. The believers were on the hill, firm soul-holds; the unbelievers were on slippery grounds, shifty. But then, just as victory was in sight the believers let go the firm-words of Muhammad Al-amin for the shifty dazzling booties of the unbelievers... Will believers this time round leave the kawlul-amin, the words of the trustworthy, for the illusionary booties of the unbeliever?'

Guard your story, said The Preacher, it's the only part of you that lasts. Yes, bones rot, heart, brain, everything rots, but the story is immortal, it's the soul that lives in the hell or heaven of our memories.

'What do you mean?' Younger Brother asked.

'Exactly that' said The Preacher, 'we bless Ruhu-llah and Katim-anbiya because of their stories; likewise the story of Yazid and broad-nape Shamiri make good people call The- God/ess's wrath upon them...'

What did Yazid and broad-nape Shamiri do?

Ah, so you don't know? Let me tell you: They murdered Hussein ibn Ali on the Mounts of Kaibara; they starved him and his faithful band of water in that fiery place; they tried to stop the eternal spring of Kawtharr from flowing. The story is shameful, so shameful; the majority of the middle nation does not like to listen to it; but a

67

minority wants it over the loud speakers. Attitudes to that story are at the heart of the split between the Sunni and the Shia of the middle nation, Islam, dinullah.

But I haven't guarded my story well. I dunked my hands into my insides and remove a bloody heart (but who hasn't a bloody heart? Did the scientist not say the heart is the circulator of bloody things?). Once I buried a dog alive; inside its damned mouth I put a list of the doomed persons of my hope and buried all in a nightly earth. My story was running amok, knocking down my better hopes, fracturing the cranium of my dreams, maddening them. I sacrificed the dog to save my story...

The story of my dying is the story of a dog being buried alive, with the fate of others sewn into its tongue. This tongue can't touch the roof of the mouth, dirt separates them, the tongue can't tell its dying because of this dirt – too much dirt in the channels of telling.

The othertime it was Duramani's bony wife, Thuma, the virgin, remember, from the forest held down by us for Brother Duramani's phallus. The child she got from that marital rape was famishing, its fate that of a rat in a gathering of cats.

'Witches,' Thuma cried. She took out her only hen, transubstantiated it into a witch, pierced her with forty needles and burnt her alive.

Cousin Duramani said 'mate, that fowl knew how to die... it didn't say a word, nor did it grumble or flail its

68

wings in useless protest. It just stared into the gossipy crowd cheering its fall and fell.'

'But why,' I asked, 'why Brother Duramani, why did you allow Thuma to do it?'

'To assuage her pain, her child was dying.'

'But you knew it was superstition, useless.'

'Yes, the child died, everything we do is worthless, we can't stop death...'

'But that was evil. Anyway you look at it, roasting a fowl alive is evil.'

'Momodu, let me tell you what I've gone through...I was just like you... Mine was a heart-ful of tears watering the fields of our sadnesses – evergreen, ever young; I never allowed my sadness to mellow out. I was a very committed gardener of sadnesses, a man who freely gave barns of unhappiness to all.

But one day, an old man, by all account a good man who had been receiving my sheaves of sadness called me aside, 'Beloved,' he said, 'the pot of what we call life stands on three stones; one stone is called good, the other evil and the third hypocrisy. The day any one of these is removed shall be the end of life.'

'No father,' I cried, 'I want life, life, life.'

69

'Then don't waste your precious youth crying over evil, it's an equally important prop of the illusion we call life.'

'But father you're a good man, so good, feeding orphans, sheltering displaced, getting people off the gutters of our anguish.'

'It's instinctual beloved, ingrained in my being. I don't do what I'm doing to remove evil... only doing it because I love doing it, doing it makes me feel happy. If I had hated doing it, I would've stopped.'

'What?'

'Yes beloved, I want to be happy; I'm not put here to cry over cats eating mice, what use it is to ask for the age of an aborted fetus? To celebrate its birthday, or perhaps deathday? What can we do when water is spilled on sand? Recover it? We are but base fluids big-banged onto the exploding expanse of nothingness. Do you act to catch your breath in this forced marathon where the winners' trophy is death and nothingness, and the losers' consolation prizes are also death and nothingness? The breath of life itself is the nothingness blown into you by Hesheit that was before our beginning. Ask your astronomers; the stars are moving away from us, the guiding lights are speeding away. Are you still staring at the stars darting away from us? When you catch your breath, it is nothingness, when you speed on, it is unto nothingness.
'Give a damn beloved; act yourself reflexively, what ever it is... fill the emptiness that you've been propelled unto by the forces that be; that's the only way to hurry through this side of nothingness.

'Yes beloved, ruminating over actions wastes your time, the reflexes don't. Reason stalls your un-being, reasoning prolongs your exile this side of nothingness, reasoning hinders your returning home to the better nothingness we come from.

'Yes beloved, consciousness is painful, it's an excrescence that poisons our happiness; it's the harbinger of conscience- that seat of venomous remorse that kills our hilarity.'

'Our lives, you mean?'

'Yes beloved, but calling it life deceives you into thinking that it's stable, but since it's not, and the evidence is all around, the name creates a dichotomy between what you feel and what really is. That dichotomy is the source of your anguish.'

'What then would you have me call it, living?'

'That's worse. This is because it posits the wrong notion of life as growing, adding itself unto itself, like sediments to form mountains... No, beloved, calling it living deepens the anguish. I'd rather call it dying, a returning home from exile, home sweet home...'

'But father, would we not hasten the return by fighting evil, removing one of the stones on which this painful illusion rests?'

'You can as well hasten our return by seeking to uproot good or hypocrisy, the illusion equally rests on them.'

71

'What's hypocrisy father?'

'Hating to do what's instinctual to you, so you're a medley of what you're and what you think you should be, a two-face being continually crying to yourself and the world...'

'But what if that which you feel, that which is your instinctual is evil; and you strive to uproot it'

'The instinctual can't be removed...'

'But it can be moderated, curbed.'

'Then you become a hypocrite...'

'But one for good, one weighted in favor of the good...'

'But still a hypocrite, always cussing his lapses; remorseful, unhappy, and it becomes worse when you an extreme hypocrite, for the sadness increases, and now you loathe those who carry the cross of their existence with poise and equanimity, with laughter, with knowledge that life is just not worth painful exertions. Why should you allow the cross of your death to be wounding you shoulders as you carry it to your Golgotha?'

'Throw it away then, father'.

'Hahaha, the cross is within, you cannot throw away the cross of the genetic prophesy of our ascension unto the other side of nothingness.'

'Hmmm,' Duramani exclaimed after narrating this encounter with the old man, 'there's much truth in what that good Pa told me... Yes Momodu, our firmaments are nothingness-laden, death ever-drizzling down our skulls...'

'Well then,' I replied, 'we must build roofs against it.'

'Where do you stand whilst building a roof in this rain, is it not in the rain? Lo, you turn your back to it to build the roof...'

'But it can be done... and if I die others will continue.'

'It's useless, mate, roofs can't hold it out. It's a photon-rain, a wave nothing can stop, it's in your blood, brain, everywhere... what do you want to build the barricade against? It's not outside you; the rain is your memory, your story, it's you, the rain is you, you're death-drizzling, you're a dying... come on, acknowledge it, embrace your dying, it's the way to happiness...'

'I'm a believer in The-God/ess, I won't embrace a philosophy that leaves out The-God/ess.'

'This is not a philosophy or logic; it's a feeling, a feeling made known. And The-God/ess is not out of it, The-God/ess is The Not, The Great Nothingness, indescribable even in its indescribability.'

Inside me it was like I was hearing The Preacher say: Islam's first word – la - is a negation. The very first sentence of the faith reads –la –no; illah – god; ila – except; llah – The Deity. Or as some exegetes say, the Wow, so indescribable that it erodes all thoughts except lla, or wow. This primal exclamatory indescribability is the exception to the nothingness. But to except is to negate. The Deity is a negation of the negation, it is a negation, a nothingness; nothing exists but the negation of nothingness.

'Yes,' I heard Duramani say outside me, 'embracing your dying is the true way to The-God/ess...'

'Cousin Duramani,' I said, 'now that I know that you don't fear death, why must we not gang up to stop the many nonsenses in this country...'

'It's useless,' he replied.

(Now I think I must interrupt this flow to draw your attention to Duramani's love for the phrase 'it's useless' in his philosophy, sorry, feeling of uselessness... but I must go on with the story).

'...It useless,' he replied, 'pouring your blood on the pond to stop the larva from breathing is outright stupid; the larva have long become mosquitoes pushing malarial parasites into our every endeavor, there are more mosquitoes in the world than humans...'

74

'What's us if we don't stand up against the rot?'

'What rot, the one in the fields, of the crops that could not be harvested. Hey, they ferment, become alcoholic liquids that send us on high. Remember what that drunken American writer said, 'fermentation is the beginning of civilization.' Fermentation brings in the happiness of the tavern. Bring on the belles, bring on the bottle, pump the music. Did Khayyam not say his heaven is to be with a woman and a bottle of wine near a running stream? Did Omar the Tent Maker not tell us to experience the divine by staining our prayer rugs with wine? So let things rot, let things ferment, let the river flow. Not standing up against the rot brings easy dying, painless dying. But you, you won't have that... It's all because of your addiction to this remorse-stimulant called conscience... Mate, that's not the dope to enjoy your dying.'

'Cousin Duramani, I don't like em em this your give-a-damn feeling about the world, it's like the crushed hugging the boots crushing them.'

'What if being a solid manifestation is the painful temporal quality that needs to be crushed into its original blissful void- like quality, would you call the crushing evil?'

Younger Brother butted in, 'so you like to be trampled upon, kicked, crushed, without resisting, without putting a fight, a heroic show of life.'

75

'You're getting me wrong. Look, if it's instinctual to fight back, why not, I'll fight against being crushed if I feel that way at the moment of crushing... What I'm saying is the basis for actions should be feelings, the instinctual. If I feel being crushed is a painful way of dying, I'll fight to get my sweet way. You get me, I'll fight for a sweet dying, it's far better than fighting to defend this mirage called life or living.'

I asked, 'but what do you do if you are prevented from dying?'

'I'd like to meet that tyrant who keeps people in obeisance by threatening them with life...'

'I mean your type of dying, what if people prevent you from sowing your randy seeds in every mulch?'

'Smug, won't you learn... my dying is a give-a-damn affair...it's fearless, a truly dying person fears nothing, for he knows that in the end nothing really counts. So he laughs at those who seek to impose their will on others, and also those upon whom the will of others are imposed...He knows it's their fear of their dying that causes that. No man, laugh the tyrant's exertions, it is futile, it ends in the grave... laugh the futile exertions mate, real give-a-damn laughter unmakes the tyrant and makes you happy in the straight jacket environment.'

Duramani was laughing the limbs of my dying faith in life and the divine the way a cat laughs the dying limbs of a rat; the cat wants to gobble the rat but it must have fun awhile. Duramani wanted to gobble my faith, but it was not yet dead, also it was not alive... O me O my precursors in fiction. In Hamidou Kane's *Ambiguous Adventure,* Samba Diallo wouldn't pray, wouldn't un-pray; in Salman Rusdie's *Midnight Children,* Aadam Aziz wouldn't believe, wouldn't un-believe in The-God/ess. O man in a haze, not knowing, for instance, how to address his cousin Duramani, sorry mother said I should call him brother, that cousin is un-African; sorry, for Duramani would rather have me call him Duramani, brother or cousin before name too old fashion; sorry, I wouldn't, for Duramani is older than me, it would be disrespectful on my part to just call him that... O me O me...

'Do you have that laugh?' it was cousin, sorry brother sorry, Duramani, sorry, it was him, 'two Fridays ago my instinct just pushed me into a mosque and The Preacher was saying, 'there are two angels who have been laughing since their creation. Do you know what they're laughing at? One's laughing at those who don't want what The-God/ess wants; their efforts are futile. The other is laughing at the futile exertions of those who want what The-God/ess does not want... Momodu, I've become these angels long ago, I'm a bundle of mirth.'

Younger Brother also, when he lived (Get off me tale mate, I have promised you in the very first pages that I

77

will tell you his death later) nothing, for him, was beyond laughter. While Papa way dying I was at a meeting talking book, quoting Socrates. Younger Brother went to call me. Back home we met Papa already dead and mother was hollering, 'he was hot he was hot so hot he was hot so hot.' Everybody was crying. Not Younger Brother; mother's 'he was hot so hot' crunched him into a ball of laughter rolling about our fields of sorrow.

Later that night, I cussed his unfeeling being; his ungratefulness to the memory of the man who fed, clothed and sheltered him. 'No,' he remonstrated, 'I was hurt by Papa's death, but mother's 'he was hot he was hot' was just funny; I was laughing at the way she expressed her hurt.'

Ways of expressing hurt: every new mourner came with her own ululation and mother would reply 'he was hot so hot,' and the chorus of mourning soprano/falsetto/tremble/tenor/twang would chorus 'patience O be patient sister/aunt/child/mother.' And the new mourner would join the chorus, their lamentation tailing off now until another mourner came with her own idiosyncratic dirge and mother would 'he was hot so hot' and the chorus would...

Not only that, Papa's laying out was a moment of thousands of stories and messages. 'Go tell your brother my father,' said a cousin to the corpse, 'that things are difficult out here. Rebels burnt down the compound and we are all displaced now. Tell him that it was good he died before the war, for everything he toiled for in this world was destroyed. Tell him his third wife disappeared when our village was attacked. We do not know whether she had joined him over there or she is lost somewhere in the forest.'

'Go tell your sister my mother,' said another, 'that her grand daughter my child had her arms amputated, her two arms.'

'Go tell your uncle my grand father, that his son is now a drug addict. He got the habit when he became a rebel and was forced to kill his own sister. He is now half mad, threatening everyone with death.'

'Go tell our people over there that times are hard; a bag of rice is unaffordable; prices of basic commodities are going up; thieves now have guns, they don't hide to steal, rather they point their guns at you and before your very face take away your sweat.'

WOMAN-VISITOR AND THE REVOLT OF THE YOUNG

Exactly two hours after the telling of the family happenings, Papa's corpse no coffin, but with lots of stories, rolled on the waves of our tears... (no, not tears, for only women shed tears at funerals, which is why they aren't allowed at Muslim corpse-dumping... tears, if you don't know, are faggot-like on the skin of corpses, hurt them too much) So two hours after the telling of the family, with no women around, papa's corpse no coffin rolled on the waves of our dirge to the shores yonder. We wished it a safe berth yonder horizon where our little nothingness is stitched into the great nothingness.

'See,' said The Preacher at the graveside, 'this is the greatest sermon to the living; the splitting of the bowels of nothingness to hide this nothingness of a friend brother father uncle grandfather in-law. We came with nothing, we are nothing and we go with nothing. No better peace comes to us than the awareness of this truth...

'Long ago a learned and God/essly king ruled half the world. His name was Zhul-qarnain, owner of the two horns, the dual trumpets. But as death comes to all - even the best loved of creatures Katim Anbiya, the seal of the prophets, also called Muhammad did die - Zhul-qarnain was to meet his death. On his deathbed he asked that his corpse be paraded round his kingdom with his lifeless nude palms, outstretched, very visible to all.

'Why this great king,' a counselor asked. 'The learned will one day tell you,' the great king replied.

'Be done with your myths Preacher,' it was Younger Brother, 'don't waste people's time, they have to find a living, a living time and death-talk wastes living time...'

The Preacher was struck dumb; this had never happened before. Younger Brother continued, 'scientific preaching, man, short, concise, to the point...'

'Sure sure,' Sana joined in, 'talk about life, about the living organisms that are part of the corpse. Listen o listen, this is scientific, verifiable. I am a universe of organisms. Millions of other organisms subsist in me. My mouth contains millions of microbes; my stomach is a warm universe for bacteria munching the great many juices within. My anus also. So who is this me? Am I an individual? Does my universe, this universe in me stop existing because this me drops dead. Or do these million of organisms continue to exist in the places where I would be buried? I am a we. We will live beyond the death of this form you see before you. I am not talking here about the soul; I am talking about something physical; the microbes that are part of me, that will live in the grave, changing this mode of existence, continuing to exist, even to the annoyance of those who think there is

81

no life in the grave. There are lives in the grave. We will always be, nothing will be lost. Existence eternal, forever.

The young men supported Younger Brother and Sana; they drowned the declining voices of the old with their yowl, 'point, point, point...'

O impatient youth, we want it quick, now now... O the inability to wait...Younger Brother was to die because of this, but that story must wait a while...

They said Papa died with his jowl resting on palms resting on elbows resting on the groaning arm of a chair. He was probably thinking something as he died. When we buried him a lizard jumped into the grave. We tried to get it out but couldn't, so we threw dirt on them, perhaps the lizard was gone to do research into the dying thoughts of Papa.

A man once did research into whether there's life in the grave. After connecting his headphone to a tape-recorder he pressed the record button and hid the tape-recorder in the hollow of the grave (you know those graves constructed like cesspits). But nothing could be hidden from the angels questioning corpses. On discovering the tape-recorder they gave such a shout that the headphone, eardrums and brain of our researcher exploded into a trillion specs.

O simulation of the trump of Azraeel that shall blow life out of every earthly thing. Preceding that, tumult – falling meteors, exploding suns, upturned mounts, boiling seas.
And after that, the comedy of the death of the Angel of Death. The God/ess says, 'go on Malaikalmawt, look, make sure all created things are dead.' All over the mutilated universe the Angel of Death searches, 'O God/ess my God/ess there is no life left.' 'Search Angel of Death, there's one hiding from you.' And Malaikalmawt shall search all over again scattering mounts splashing seas crunching suns rummaging galaxies making more upside down the already shattered universe, 'O God/ess my God/ess,' the angel tiredly cries, 'there's none left.' 'What about you, 'The-God/ess says, 'aren't you a created being?'
O the agonies of the last suicide. 'O God/ess my God/ess, it hurts.' The-God/ess replies, 'that was how you used to take the lives of others.'

O absence of the winged anesthetic, (for Angel Gibril will be long dead).

O painful suicide of the Angel of Death.

Then The-God/ess shall survey the nothingness around and say, where are you, the proud and haughty, where are you mounts of pride, valleys of treachery, suns of fury, waters of storm, earths of quakes, skies of thunder, hurricanes of winds, tsunamis of oceans, souls of sins, scenes of evil? None but The-God/ess herhimself shall hear herhimself, and there shall be no reply. But The-

83

God/ess wants a reply, so the resurrection, so judgment day.

O that day, judgment day, when the girl-child that was buried alive shall be asked for what crime was she slain. And then the march of Binturrasulillah, Fatima Zahra, the frail-bodied saint with the stout heart; marching with the blood-stained mantle of her murdered son, Al Hussein, seeking justice in the solemn court of al-Adil, The Just one... rings and rings of angels, then djinns, then menwomen...none shall speak save with the permission of The Omnipotent for that day belongs to hisherit... O those who made dinullah one of obeying the ruler without the qualification 'if he's just, good, honest, The- God/ess-loving'... O those who...

'Who what?' asked the ever impatient Younger Brother

'Who got so stuck to the literal that they become evil.'

'What do you mean?' I heard Younger Brother, though materially absent, asking again.

Statements change from literal truth to metaphorical truth. Now, in this age, literal truths mainly belong to scientific statements, but as these statements age, yes, statements do grow old; they become metaphorical truths. This has long become the case with the greatest statements contained in the holy books. Religious statements have become metaphorical truths; those stuck to their literariness unwittingly commit evil. Must we cut hands, must we stone the adulterer, must we kill the apostate? O ye who believe, why shouldn't we move on to the metaphorical renditions of those instructions?

Because they are instructions; instructions are precise, not metaphorical. The word must not be licentiousness; else we become hecklers, hypocrites, munafiquun

No, no, no, hypocrisy lies in the heart, not in the word or action. Remember Habibullah, the beloved of The-God/ess when he said, 'actions are but intentions.' Remember the Kitabul Huda, 'where ever you turn there is the face of The- God/ess.' O ye who believe, remember what the woolen ones say: 'there are as many ways to The-God/ess as there are human souls.' Shouldn't we cover our nudity with hearts, rather than with leaves?

The Preacher replied, the metaphorical can't instruct, can't guide us in the world of details, and that is the world that we live our lives.

I answered, heshe who suffers a soul unto instructions for every little thing takes that person for a fool. But The-God/ess did not create us stupid; hisherit sagacious breath is within us...

The Preacher said, you are twisting the interpretations, you are twisting the words, you are a poet, and the Kitabul Huda curses poets

I asked, but to which end do I twist the words, what's the intention?

To cause mischief, The Preacher replied.▉May The-God/ess save us from mischief makers.

Amen

Get to the centre of it, said Younger Brother, metaphors are nothing but ways of making the stupid look sensible. Parables and proverbs are the worst type, for they make these old people look wise and sensible. The old no longer have the energy to practically search out for the truth, so they sit there, and mouth metaphors, and tell us it is the truth about the world. Metaphors are the ropes around necks that the old use to control us. Be done with metaphors, proverbs and parables.

But you are using metaphors to bring down metaphors.

You use iron to cut iron, Younger Brother replied.
God/ess purpose, said Sana, moves in ways we know not. That's why priests are now at the helm of the great deception. The priests think they are the party of The God/ess; Satan thinks so too, so he sends his venom unto them, leaving untouched the real vice-regents of God/ess, the new caliphs, the kulapha, the menwomen of science, the people of the door, ulul bab. Satan even draws unto himself the fire from the party of God/ess against the new caliphs. By calling scientific knowledge

carnal satanic knowledge the Party of God/ess got even
Satan to defend it. The Party of God/ess curse evolution,
stem work on stem cells in Yankee-land, deny global
warming, generally want to turn back the advance of
technology. The Lord moves in a mysterious way, even
Satan himself now defends hisherit chosen ones. So the
new caliphs move on to the glory of the lord, fulfilling
the deification of man/woman by other means – science,
technology, growth. The chosen ones are fulfilling our
mandates as co-creators, continuing the co-creative act,
multiplying, evolving us, by design into something better,
designer human beings would soon be here, longevity is
being extended, the great transformation has begun, but
few see the glory of the coming of the lord.

It shall be well with you, Sana continued. You worship
the God/ess unrecognizably. It shall be well with you.
God/ess knows calling hisher name is also a calling forth
of that which is not God/ess. So calling God/ess name
may no longer be necessary. Doing the work is better,
you banish God/ess and the non-god from the
vocabulary. You think not in terms of the God/ess-non
God/ess divide. You just do the good thing, the
institutions are geared towards ensuring happiness, the
good life, the good, humanity. We speak about the good
in secular terms. That is like doing God's work, humanity
fulfills its mission, fulfills itself, becomes perfect, that is
the meaning of the returning on to God/ess. Glory be to
the God/ess.

Anyway let me leave aside those megalomaniac propositions and me continue with the story of the lizard, the one that went into Papa's grave; what was it fate? Did it get the knowledge it was looking for? Or did it choke to death? Or was it smashed into smithereens by the hammers of the Angels of the Grave, Mankirr and Manakirr?

The-God/ess forbid, the Angels of the Grave wouldn't do such a thing to a lizard. It was just a lizard, a non-manwoman, mere animal, and mere animals, said The Preacher, are unaccountable for their deeds. They won't enter heaven or hell. Next world, on the Day of Judgement, The-God/ess would just say unto them, 'be dust' and they will become dust. But evildoers will envy this dust; they will crave to be dust like the animals. But they will be denied this – hell will be lying in wait, an ambush, djinns; menwomen and stones shall be its fuel...

'Haven't you seen some stones crying,' an ignorant-always- sad fanatic once told me, 'those are the sensible ones, they know what will happen to them come judgment day, but men, ah unbelieving men, always smiling, always rollicking with passion...'

'So I should be sad?' I asked the bumpkin.

'Yes,' the skunk replied, 'sadness is next to The- God/essliness.'

Not cleanliness, for that Jahil (that's how the inhabitants of Jahiliyya, the kingdom of ignorance, are called) was filthier than an ill-ventilated ill-drained pit-latrine with a leaky roof...

Stampeding feet jolted me out of the reverie about the fate of lizards, stones and jahils. We were at the gates of the cemetery now, and corpse-dumpers were stamping their feet to get grave soils off them. The grounds round the gates of our necropolis are the most stamped upon in the world... bomp bamp bomp bamp... I too had joined the stampede bomp bamp. It was like I was avenging the soils' swallowing of my father... Bop bap...
'Wai wai ...' that was the shriek of a woman in pain but I was busy with my revenge... bop bap bop bap...

'Waiiii...' I felt something creaking under my boots. I looked down. The-God/ess! The peeled insteps of the woman white as paper, then red crisscrossing lines, like when testing the writing power of red-ink pen...

'Waiii,' the lips that cried thus were firmly set in a drearily beautiful face - little furrow mid-forehead smoothening into a dazzle between eyes twinkling with agony, nose-curves finely carved... 'waaiiiii'

I cupped her face, 'I'm sorry so sorry.'

She muttered something in a pained and hungry voice. I felt what she was trying to say but I just couldn't make it out;; her voice was an indecision between the audible and the inaudible. I stretched ear to catch a straying account.

A crowd gathered around us, someone ventured, 'the woman is dying of pain, let's carry her to the hospital.'

'No,' she whimpered in a voice I could finally make sense of, 'I'm hungry, I want something to eat.'

'What is she saying?' an interloping corpse dumper asked.

'Help me carry her home; we have plenty of what she needs at our house.'

Most parts of our house were collapsing - perforated ceilings, crater-floor, displaced latches, rickety jambs, mossy foundation on eroding soils.

'We've done it,' said The Preacher, he was continuing the after-burial sermon at our house. 'We've opened the belly of the earth to dump a man we all love. Do you know why we did that, why we dumped a man we love? Strange, but it's because we hate what he has become. We love him but what he has become would rot in our hands, make our homes foul scented.
'It was not a shameful thing that we did. In fact what we did was to cover his rot, his shame and our embarrassment. The Holy Recitations, also called the

Tanzil, that which is sent down, in the story of Kabila and Habila calls the corpse a shame, and that even a criminal like Kabila also called Cain, a brother-slayer, did cover the shame of his brother... At first he did not know what to do with the murdered brother, so he toted him wherever he wandered, maggots dripping on his soul. Then he saw two ravens fighting; one killed the other, and started scratching the earth. Then the living raven put the dead raven in the scratched soil and covered it. Ah so that's the way to do it, exclaimed Cain. Yes, a raven taught him that; yes, everything has its purpose in creation, a raven, superstitiously despised, taught humanity the art of dumping brothers sisters aunt child...'

'Like they did to my one year old girl, they dumped her in a swamp alive... O it's not that hard to leave behind a dead kin, but an ill-dead one...'

The-God/ess! It was the voice of the woman I stepped upon giving an account of the existence of Jahiliyya, the pre- prophet Muhammad Meccan practice of burying alive the girl- child.

The woman held up the ball of rice she had molded for her mouth and flung it at the gown of The Preacher. '...that was how he did it, flung my girl to the unfeelingness of this earth.'

The unfeeling earth was The Preacher and she rushed at him, grabbed him the grabbing of a strong one, eyes

91

popping out like those of an enlarged drawing of a housefly in a biology text, 'where's my child, my child where did you leave my child?'

The corpse dumpers or mourners or shame-dumpers darted towards her, the way a chameleon's tongue darts to snap an insect. They twisted her arms, kicked, cussed her. I dashed too, to wrench her from them, 'she's my visitor, my visitor,' I barked, biting the calves of their murderous resolve... They gave way and I carried the bleeding woman to my room...

Room now, I placed her on my bed the way a new mother places her baby in a cot, and fired out like a bullet to the kind heart of a dispenser-friend. I shattered it into specs of grief – this kind heart of this short man with a tonsure shine-oily like palm-oil on kwashiorkor belly. He said he didn't have drugs or bandages; nonetheless he came with me.

We met my visitor slithering with Duramani or cousin Duramani in the pus of her sore-memories. 'That was why I attacked The Preacher, he was boasting about having dumped a person, just like that rebel who flung away my child. My child hadn't eaten for two days in the bushes of the rebels' tortuous march, and she was crying her guts out on my back. The rebel said my child was making too much noise; so he wrenched her from my back and flung to bog. When I turned to retrieve her he hit me with the butt of his gun and yelled, 'march, bloody civilian.'   ... It's hard, hard to leave behind a dead kin, but a dying child, your own child...'

Sana once wrote a poem about being an un-bloody civilian:

I'm a civilian,
Though not as military men say, a bloody civilian.
I'm a bloodless civilian,
a cockroach; I love books,
I sulk in night corners
 afraid of the light
that illuminates the books.
I read in the gloom,
the gloom the doom of the closet teaming with my mind,
yea not my heart
 but my kind – maggots rats bugs.
I'm a roach,
I know my place.
Lacking blood I don't interfere in a butchers' palaver.
I hate guns,
goons with guns gunning gutter guys dock
 – ing further down into the piss to save head –
more peaceful than split skulls drying teeth under the sun.

Anyway let's leave Sana alone and continue with our story. Woman visitor said, 'It's hard, hard to leave behind a dead kin, but a dying child, your own child...'

93

Dispenser-friend, poor in real bandages and drugs, cleaned the woman's sores with the cotton and antiseptic of his heart, 'have faith sister, this is but to test your faith.'

'If faith comes only through suffering, I'd rather unfaith and no suffering.' Duramani said this bitterly, like my aunt did to the 'soak' she met shaving my balls, 'what do you want his pubic hair for, do you want to turn him into a hen-pecked man?'

'No maam,' the 'soak' replied, 'just a way to show how I love him.'

Dispenser-friend was as taken aback by the outburst of Duramani or brother Duramani as were the Bedouin Muslim conquerors at seeing the carpets of the seventh century kings of Persia, eyes sparking with disbelief at the floored splendor, mouths curving into Os of wonder at the genius of Zarathustra's compatriots...

But there is a better simulacrum: dispenser-friend was Al-Ghazali tormented by the splendid nothingness of the poetry of Umar-al-Khayyam:

You have seen the world and what you saw was nothing
All you have said and heard; that is nothing
Running from pole to pole; there was nothing
And when you lurked at home; there was also nothing

Duramani continued, 'suffering teaches no lesson, it does not make sufferers better or anything, sufferers will make others suffer if they have the chance.'

Sometimes I feel Duramani or cousin Duramani or... is The- God/essdamn right. Anguish teaches nothing; the world sort of T.S Elliot's (what it him, I don't care) Men on Horseback... Just give us the chance and we'll out-Herod all known villains in life and fiction... Perhaps it has got to do with this irresistible urge to avenge one's woes... One does not want to be the last one, one wants to do unto others what others have done unto one. One does not have the strength to make it stop at one; one must pass on the baton; one shouldn't be the last one... the continuing evolution of pain must not stop with one; pain must progress until it becomes the much talked about hell, lake of sulphur —that's the fulfillment of the reverse-divine. That's the meaning of the end of history for those on the losing side. Hell eternal, the perfection of exterminating of all but the liberal democratic ideal. That's the meaning of the Hegelian triumphalism for those on the wrong side of Fukuyama's closure of history.

'It's all toiletese, fugues of the same old fart,' said Duramani or... 'This rationalizing or moralizing of suffering... they have no hold on the impulses of the moment.'

Is cousin Duramani or... a re-incarnation of Umar al-Khayyam who seeing the wastage wrought on his country by Mongols became a poetic indecision between faith and unfaith? But perhaps Cousin Duramani or...is only an extension of me the present autobiographer, another part of me in argument with another part of me; a fiction-shadow cast by the real me... Me me me, a starving migrant craving the pagan- skewed but divinely tolerated treaty of Hudaibiya…

What is the treaty of Hudaibiya? Younger Brother asked.

Eee, so you don't know about the Treaty of Hudaibiya? Okay let me tell you: Abu Ibrahim and his companions went to Mecca to perform their religious duties, but the Qureish refused them entry that year, and got a treaty that did not recognize the Deity as Compassionate and Merciful, that did not recognize Abu Ibrahim as a prophet of the Deity. But Abu Ibrahim accepted it. For the sake of peace, Abu Ibrahim restrained the fanatics and extremists on his holy side, and the verse of victory was given on that mantle of moderation and compromise that later got the middle nation to perform its religious rites in peace and equanimity. Have you not heard the recitations, 'the unbelievers planned, and the Deity planned, and the Deity is the best of planners'?

Anyway, let me continue with my musing: Me me me, a starving migrant craving the seemingly pagan- skewed but divinely tolerated treaty of Hudaibiya… yea, a migrant from one-God/ess-Medina to idol-filled-Mecca, lolling in the desert between these two cities...

But perhaps I'm only fiction, a lie told by someone who is a lie told by someone who is...

But what about dispenser-friend? Is he Al-Ghazali the Sufi mystic, the greatest interpreter of the Ayyatul-nur, the Verse of the Light.

The-God/ess is the Light of the Heavens and the Earth. Those who behold himherit without veils cast no shadow; Light upon Light upon Light, waves upon waves upon waves of joyous light, those who behold himherit without veil cast no grave, no tomb, the earth's core can not claim them. For they subsist on light, they are light, they cast no shadow.

But who is responsible for the veil? Between us and The-God/ess is the veil, who is responsible for it? Who put that veil between the Deity and us? asked Younger Brother.

There are two sides to the veil. On The-God/ess' side the veil is a curvature around our spec of an earth, a mercy, an ozone, else ill-prepared eyes/perceptions/beings will be hurt without it; on our side the veil is a weakness, it is the lack of discipline to scale the gravitation pulling our perceptions to the dark fire of the earth's core, it is the lack of the astronomer's urge to peer beyond the horizons of the earth, the vision is earthbound, the veil is the earthboundness of our dispositions, the absence of faith, of love, of desire to behold the infinite expanse of the Beautiful One.

Therefore pray: O Beautiful One grant my perception the velocity to escape its earthboundedness, grant me strength to remove my veil

97

that covers my face from Yours, O The- God/ess I seek your face, your radiance, O love O love, I seek the radiance of Your beauty. O Beautiful One, O loving One, al Wadud, an-Nur, az-Zahir, grant us the brilliance of your Manifest; grant us the strength to remove our veil that covers our faces from yours, prepare us for the rupture of the veil, O al-Wadud, O The-God/ess, We seek your face, your radiance, O love O love, We seek the radiance of your beauty, make us members of the realm of your eternal sufficiency.

We were created to behold beauty. The-God/ess is beauty, but there is none to behold hesheit. So hesheit created us to behold hisherit beauty. To be human is to behold beauty. Heshe who cannot behold beauty is not human. O Beautiful one, make me fulfil the purpose of my creation. Fulfill the purpose of your creating me, O beautiful One, make me see you.

We are the signs of the Beautiful One, the beauty of The- God/ess is within us. Heshe who distorts this beauty is against The-God/ess. Therefore pray, May we behold the Beautiful One. But you should first start with the signs of hisherit beauty. The signs are everywhere, and only they who behold them fulfill the purpose of their creation. We fulfill creation when we behold and wonder. The best form of prayer is the beholding of beauty. Fill your sights with joy; dance to the rhythm of your inner beauty. Mine the divine diamonds deep inside your beings. Hang them about your actions. May your doings sparkle with the beholding of beauty. Be beautiful.

But what bloody diamonds those are, said Younger Brother, should we butcher guts to look for swallowed diamonds, should we mine diamonds in the rivers of blood. Tell me tell me I have seen it with my own eyes in the killing fields of Bamakonta, the butchery, the oubliettes of oddities, the graves of greed, the tombs of toil, the wombs of woes, I have seen it all, I have seen it all.

You mixing divinity with depravity, I thundered.
I am asking questions. I have a questioning voice. My speech is naturally interrogative. And to remind you, the question about dispenser friend is still not answered, said Younger Brother.

Okay impatient youth, Okay cynical Younger Brother, thank you for reminding me. The question is: Is dispenser friend this Al Ghazali, now a displaced in time and place, wrought out of context like African masks in the art-galleries of Europe, like mummies in European museums, like castaway Hajara also called Hagar in the deserts of Arabia, flabby breasts flapping hollow stomach in the rugged hills of Safa and Marwa, running up and down those divine mounts till soul-tired she saw hope gushing ground under her half-caste son's flailing feet. That gushing legend is the holy Zamzam well near The-God/ess' house at Bekka also called Mecca whose foundations were laid by that half-caste that nearly died and his Aryan father, Abul-anbiya, father of the prophets, also called Anabi-Brima before which he was known as Abram of Ur.

'House, house, house... to build a house,' said the metaphor-mad coordinator of a creative writing workshop, 'you need mortar; you need spades, and

99

men/women, and a plan, in your head, or on paper. Same-wise a poem or essay or novel or play; you need paper(s), you need a pen or typewriter or computer, and words and a heart, warm and penetrating.

'Be marvelous, let manwoman wonder at the way wee words wander on the infertile manuscript, at how we make the arid page blossom forth with all things beautiful, roses; with all things ugly, brambles.

'Sometimes the words fall heavy, than August rain, and people, like goats and sheep huddling together under one roof for fear of the rain, wonder, butt one another, why this vehemence, inscrutable, inscrutable, whence this anger?

'Othertimes the diction is thunderous, glowing sky-crevices fight each other, cancel out each other and lo! The one who stole grandma's fowl is frightened.

'This time the words are dancing, enjoying themselves, gyrating to the beat of the imaginative heart... a serenade here, on this esplanade strewn with rosy stories, won't you throw confetti to the writer.

'Creative writing is a leisurely stroll with ideas (and emotions) along the lanes of experience. Not always: sometimes it's not a leisurely stroll, the path is thorny, the ideas are naughty, they make faces at you, make you angry, you trip over, fall and bruise the softer parts of your soul... you cry, you wail, you holler your anguish, and the readers are sympathetic. Not always, plentytime they laugh at the way you cry, it's funny; they hold their bellies and laugh till they fall on the ground.

'Write, write, write there's always something to write with; the ink of experience is always there. Are you afraid of inkblots – those messy things that dishearten?'

Inkblots, the coordinator's mention of inkblots propelled me to my class six years. Something important crept into our headmaster's cranium and he decreed, 'henceforth all class five six and seven children must use fountain pen.'

Fountain pens? Our parents bought us the pens and the inkbottles or fountains, from the school of course; our headmaster insisted on that. But we never mastered the use of the pens. Inkblots on paper and fingers; blood blots on fingers and our class five six seven backs, both at home and school. (I tell you, school days could only be best when remembered through adult eyes; the foibles make you laugh). The beatings only stopped when the headmaster's supply of pen and ink stopped. And then also did we, little children as we were, know the something important that went into our headmaster's cranium – the noise of ill-sharing of the donor-loot between headmaster and teachers dinned into our tiny heads the money-factor of our agony.

But now I must leave these childhood distractions and move on to better things, to what The Preacher said,

101

'The-God/ess is the ultimate other, moving towards Himherit is moving out of oneself to that other, and what better praxis of that than loving your neighbor than yourself. For your neighbor is The- God/ess's image; but you're also The-God/ess's image, this otherness lurks inside you, and so travelling towards the other is in reality travelling towards yourself... the otherness of your very selfhood.'

'Where is the self?' Younger Brother asked The Preacher, 'point me the self, what is the seat of the self.'

'You are very rude,' I told Younger Brother, 'you don't talk to a Preacher like that.'

But Duramani or cousin Duramani or ... cut me short... 'no, it is preachers that are rude... in a very special way mate. Now the most despicable words religious people have are unbelievers, pagans, Kafiri, hypocrite. So when a religious person calls you an unbeliever or hypocrite, know he's abusing you in the most damn way. And that's exactly what they always do in churches and mosques; but nobody calls them rude - their expletives are holy talk...

'And great many times preachers talk mournfully, as if The- God/ess is dead, and they're reading the will of the dead Deity...With themselves as the greatest inheritors, and administrators of what ever accrues to others, since others, for them, are minors...

102

'And they are quick, ah so quick to intimidate people with hell. There was this preacher who was telling people about how every adulteress would on judgment day tote every man they had committed adultery with and bring them to their husbands. A women in the congregation asked The Preacher, but sir, what if I come with my adulterer but meet my husband being carried away by an adulteress to her husband?

The Preacher did not expect this type of question, and he said to the women, 'that question could only come from a hell- bound woman.'

The word 'hell' made me writhe in pain. 'Shut up!' I shouted at Duramani. Now anytime Duramani remonstrated against preachy people he became ugly, like the scrotum of a sickly man. Make no joke about it, a sick man's shriveling scrotum about one of the ugliest things on earth...

You are too vulgar, said Salifu.

Everybody is privately vulgar, I say

But that is why we cover the private in public to spare ourselves vulgarity

Being vulgar in public is a sign of one's confidence, said Duramani, it is a show of one's don't-worrying nature. Vulgarity is an indicator of one's primal freedom.

103

Hahaha, laughed Sana, let those who worry about oral vulgarity also worry about physical vulgarity of our lives. Vulgarity to the ears should be as important as vulgarity to the ears.

Anyway let me leave this discussion about themes and shades of vulgarity and continue with my tale. 'The men,' it was my woman visitor, 'thrust their penises into my unprepared vulva. I couldn't secrete enough water inside me to ease the friction, so their penises peeled the linings, peeled them like hell, blood oozed out of me but still they came.'

The word 'hell' made me writhe in dual dolor, the pain of remembered-papa-whacking-for-drinking-wine made me feel her pain like it was done to me...

'A man saved me from them, one of their own, just like you did, he dashed into their midst and wrenched me from their penises.'

Duramani; or cousin Duramani or...got out after I shouted him down. I told dispenser- friend that I would go get some money for bandages. I dived into papa's funeral fund and took out some money. I gave dispenser-friend; he went out to buy the things....

THE COCK AND THE GOD/ESS

Someone was shrieking outside like a hog in pain. I dashed out. It was an old woman, a relative, my grandaunt, one of those displaced by the war. She was hollering, 'no no, I heard it, I heard my name, you want to sell me....'

It all started when she heard her name on the radio obituary notice of my father. Not understanding the language of the announcement she thought they were putting up an advertisement about her - a woman named Yeabu Thorlie is for sale... 'leave me leave me I heard my name, you want to sell me...'

When the war brought her to Romeron, she put up with a cousin who owned a beautiful house in the country outskirts of town. But the old woman just couldn't bring herself to shit in the toilet inside the house, 'it's unclean to shit under the roof you lay your head'. So she did it in the bushes and the posh neighbors didn't particularly like it; so she had to be brought to our house where the roof where she slept was not the same with the roof under which she defecated. And, of course, there were no bushes around.

But here she was always yelling; she had this feeling about people plotting against her. She read every move with apprehension, and worse for her, people always put up shows to taunt her suspicions. The othertime they said her name was in the newspaper. Ever since a cousin of hers was hanged for treason, and the cousin's photo put in a newspaper, she had always associated newspapers with death. So she hollered, 'no, no, no, I've done nothing wrong, nothing wrong.'

What is treason? Asked Younger Brother.

It is the bad luck of being in the bad books of bad politicians; it is the bad luck of adopting unsuccessful methods of removing them. So you are tried by a friend of the bad politicians; so you are found guilty by a jury of relatives of the bad politicians; so you are hanged, acid poured on your corpse and then you are buried in an unmarked grave; so your relatives are barred from mourning you; so your spouse is harassed to penury; so memories of you are locked up in prisons of fear; they never see the liberty of day until the bad politicians dies: that, beloved is treason.

'I've done nothing wrong,' hollered my grand-aunt, 'my name is in no paper, tell me Momodu, is my name in the paper?'

Younger Brother asked, why should you say grandaunt, and not just grandmother, which is what we call sisters of our mothers' mothers?

Sana replied, it is difficult at one-go to shun a language of its privileged expressions, even if your mission has within it a liberating ethos. Momodu has tried a lot to liberate the language he uses from the stranglehold of sexism and other imprimatur of oppression, exploitation, racism or insensitivity. But hey, a balance between fair expressions and comprehensibility is most times necessary.

Comprehensibility by who? Younger Brother asked again. Whose comprehensibility do you value?

Momodu, Sana called, the question is for you.

I don't know, I replied. I have a general picture, but the specifics of the features of the faces of the persons are hard to pin down. Anyway, let me continue with the tale of my grand-aunt or grandmother:

'I've done nothing wrong,' hollered my grandaunt, 'my name is in no paper, tell me Momodu, is my name in the paper?'

My grandaunt or grandmother trusted me. I didn't know why, but the soonest she saw me she felt safe. I was the safe where she saved for her fare back home. She wanted to go home. She had told her people that many times, but they had only laughed at her, 'what with this war going on, we won't allow you.' So she confided in me; she would run away when she had saved enough for the fare. Every cent she had she gave me; every cent she gave me I bought her sweets. She loved confectioneries; she could be seen in corners sucking and sucking and she would say to me, 'Momodu, your good bye to me when leaving your town should be a carton of sweets'.

I would reply, shouting, 'when your fare is full?'

'Don't shout; this is a secret'.

And I would curve my mouth into a silent okay.

When dispenser-friend came with the bandages he met the granny clasping me like an infant monkey its mother jumping from tree to tree. They say mother monkey does not tell her child to hold tight; she just says, 'young chap, look down and see where you may fall as I jump with you'. And oh, the child would clamp her tight for dear life. That was how dispenser- friend met that granny clamping me. And granny seeing the bandages in the hands of dispenser-friend thought they were the special ropes to tie her up. She clasped me tighter; the way a drowning person clasps the reed of her dream-salvation...

'That's me, a reed thrown to the raging sea of incomprehension to save you from the void of amnesia'. That was what Prof Rainbow alias Color-rebel said at our faces crumbling in the inconceivability of his lecture about our Themne people as coming from South Africa. It all has to do with this fact of Themne belonging to the West Atlantic group of languages, which we are also told are related to Bantu languages in the Congo, which as you know is not far from South Africa, which as you know is ... Boy O girl, what is it that cannot be meaningfully stretched to mean or imply something void, utterly stupid.

'What is stupidity?'

'Nothing,' Prof Rainbow alias color rebel said, 'but statements without proper links to an original assertion. But what is it that cannot be linked by the imaginative soul?'

'Words must not be licentious,' said The Preacher, 'metaphors must be reined in, they must have bounds, else our essences behold interpretations without contexts, voids without background, we become nothing but beings that stare, we see nothing for there is nothing to see against. O Lord, how I dread metaphors without bounds. O Good Lord, save me from metaphors that link You to existences and non existences in ways that You should not linked. Deliver me from the folly of that wisdom. Guide You my metaphors, May the tents of my life be pegged to the firmness of Your purpose, spare me the agony of the void.'

Prof Rainbow alias color rebel was the greatest drunkard on campus; we also called him Bengie, which means palm wine maggot in our other language. But his all-night wine habits never got him late for his 8am lectures. He was more punctual than that German lecturer we nicknamed Herr Punklitch – Mr. Punctual. Prof Rainbow alias Colour-rebel also Bengie was very clever; you never hear wine-talk in his lectures. He was also so serious - hardly laughed. If something funny happened you'd see him fighting laughter by jerking head upwards, turning jowl to jowl, much like a cock drinking water.

They say cock once told The-God/ess he would never drink Hisherit water. Soon, however, he became very thirsty and pushed beak to pond. The-God/ess, seeing him, said, 'but cock you're drinking...' Cock replied, jerking head upwards, jowls turning this way that way, 'just this little.' Since that day he has been saying 'just this little' any time he drinks.

When Prof Rainbow alias Colour-rebel also Bengie died of wine, a brother-in wine growled, 'so, dear brother, wine has killed you, don't worry.' Brother-in-wine took a bottle of wine from his pocket and gulped everything in the funniest of all gulps, 'now wine, I've killed you too.'

Whilst dispenser friend was dressing my woman-visitor's wound, he told me this, 'I've heard more than this woman's story... One woman told me this, 'when they caught my son and I they told my son to have sex with me; he refused. So they cut his penis and choked it inside my vagina and tied it neat, neat the way a menstruating wife ties her bottom-belly to keep the blood from spilling. They didn't untie my bottom-belly until after my son's penis had rotted inside it... that's why I've come to you, dispenser, to clean my bottom-belly.'

I laughed; I hadn't meant to, by The-God/ess ...
It was embarrassing to laugh at such devilry, but I just
laughed, the thought of dispenser-friend's fingers
cleaning (which you now know also means screwing)
the woman's festering bottom-belly just made me
laugh.

Dispenser friend looked at me the way a man looks at the
rump of a baby he suspects to be defecating, 'come
woman, quick, your baby is soiling my clothes.'

The woman comes rushing, 'is he not also your baby,
and what's baby shit anyway? Besides, is it not that our
Mende people say however much a child has defecated,
his father has defecated more than him.'

The eyes of the man now show contempt bigger than
Iblisa's contempt for The-God/ess command that he
should bow down before the muck called Adam. Those
were the eyes dispenser-friend gave me that day.

'Why are you looking at me like that?' I shrieked.

'You surprise me, surprise me.' His tone was like Caesar's
when he was asking Brutus, 'et tu Brute.'

That Latin to me sounds like French for 'And you
Brute,' and you child savage, for is tu not the French
pronoun for child? Of course I know this is stretching
stuff too far; I am only joking

'I was only joking.' I answered Duramani.

'Joking,' Dispenser-Friend answered, 'people are dying and you're making fun out of it?'

'Sir, laughter dilutes pain.'

It was then that my woman-visitor laughed. You'd think it was Sarah laughing at the Man-God and her husband, Abram of Ur for planning to make her happy but without letting her into the conversation. You remember the Man-God visiting Abraham in his tent and how Sarah overheard them and laughed. 'What's this?' she asked.

'Nothing,' replied dispenser-friend, 'only talking about how to make you happy.'

'That was what the men who raped me said, 'bear it, this is only to make you happy...' and look now I'm pregnant.'

'Pregnant?'

'Yes, it's fifty-two days since I saw my last period, and that was before they raped me...'

'What do you intend to do with it?'

'What else? keep it,' she replied.

'Keep it?' I asked. I was greatly disturbed; I could just not understand why a raped woman would like to keep her pregnancy. I mean I was sort of more in sympathy with women who abort than with women who keep their pregnancies in these days of wanton child-starvation. Better send the fetus to the cesspit than send the child to the world that hollow them out into mendicant spittoon for benevolent phlegm - you see them all around; deformed skeletons wearing ragged ill-fitting skins. But this woman, she had an added reason - she was not impregnated lovingly. But here she was, vowing to keep it. It beats me; I mean the world beats me.

'And who'll take care of it? I asked.

'The Deity-on-high,' she replied, 'and myself...'

'And myself,' it was dispenser-friend, vowing to take care of woman visitor and her pregnancy.

'What? You?' I asked

'Yes me, know you not what the Furqan which in English means the Criterion says: 'kill not your children for fear of poverty.'

'But it's not yet a child.'

'It will be, and I'll father it.'

113

'Thank you,' said my woman-visitor

'Will you give it to him?'

'You wouldn't take it,' she replied

I yelled, 'what? Your pregnancy? Rebel child?'

'A woman's child also.   Mine, yours too; I could have been raped by your brother.'

My Younger Brother? Perhaps. He was a soldier, only came home when he heard Papa was sick. Could he have done that? But woman-visitor said rebels raped her, not soldiers.

'My brother is a soldier not a rebel.'

'What difference,' she cried, 'men with arms raped me... some wore uniforms, other like, you, didn't... what difference?' Her eye dam burst and gushing tears flooded her being. She choked, coughed and slumped on the bed.

Dispenser-friend darted to her mouth and chucked his mouth there, heaving like a cur on a bitch.

'What are you doing?' I shouted.

'Breathing into her, to resuscitate her...'

But to me it was like he was kissing her; and it pained me, much like it pained me when I kissed Salifu's wife and she wiped her mouth, the way some children do. You take them off the ground and kiss them and they wipe where your mouth touches theirs, like it's some foul smelling thing.

'Yes,' replied Salifu's wife, 'your mouth stinks with the after- slime of vomited words. Why did you puke to Salifu that I screwed you for a watch?'

'But it was only rum-talk, he didn't believe it.'

'But you also told Sana, not so? Man with lips that open up to any penis of an ear, man with promiscuous lips, were your lips not initiated into a secret society, must you tell my story to the whole damned world... tell me tell me what use telling me to the world?'

'Fulfilling the prophesy of my father; he told my mother that I'll become a great tale teller; but frankly speaking I don't know,' I replied.

'Don't know?' She looked at me coldly, the coldness made me judder.

'Oh Yeama,' I blubbered, 'your eyes are cold.'

'Well then never you come in front of my eyes again.'

Dispenser-friend's mouth was still in my woman-visitor's mouth. I was so annoyed that I left the room. I mean I was annoyed with my awkwardness towards women I loved. I always get too serious in wooing them, thinking very well the next word before saying it. The result was a staccato of artificiality; phrases were as mixed up as the steps of a shy woman walking a gauntlet of lustful male eyes. I didn't know how to woo women I loved.

Not so with women I sought to woo just for the sake of it. Like this woman I met in a Kingtom Poda Poda the day before Papa died:

'So we're all going to Kingtom, 'I asked her.

'Yes.' You live there?' 'Yes.'

'At the police barracks?'

'Yes'

'You're a police woman?'

'No, I'm a seamstress.'

'Where do you do your work, home?'

'No, at Bombay Street?,

'Number?'

She showed me

'Are you coming from there?'

'No, I'm coming from Wellington, from my younger
 sister?'

'How's she?'

'I didn't meet her'

'Tough luck, a wasted journey.'

'Yes.'

'But could it have been wasted of you had visited
 the guy?'

'Which guy?' She smiled.

'Lover boy, you don't have?'

'How do you see me, like one who does not
have a boyfriend?'

'I think you're virgin'

'The-God/ess forbid.'

'How old are you?'

117

'Twenty-two.'

'You're not married?'

'No.'

'Why?'

'Are you married?'

'No.'

'Why?'

'I'm looking for an unmarried woman who is not a virgin and who lives at Kingtom...'

The conversation would flow like that, without hiccups, and before disembarking I would have secured a date. Which I mosttimes missed. It all depended on my mood the date of the date. Sometimes the mood was alright and I would go to this woman who I really didn't like. I was all-brave with these women, very much my happy-go-lucky self. Also with wooing women for my friends, very successful. But with women I really loved, I was awkward, so artificial, so serious. Plentytime I would skirt around the topic until someone else snatched them from me...

I was like the man that went to borrow shoes from his friend. He didn't go straight to it; rather he started asking his friend about the weather, football and a lot of other things that gobbled up time. Then came this other guy, 'friend borrow me your shoes' He was given the shoes and our great circumlocutionist went home empty-handed...

I was like that... I always ended up not getting women I really liked... (Look, activists, I'm not equaling women and shoes by this extended metaphor; I kind of still remember the insulting arrogance of Westerners when they put up a notice at a park in China 'Dogs and Chinese not allowed.' No, mine, O fanatic, is not literary).

Rubbish, said Sana, a comparison is a comparison, there is no way you can explain away your comparison. Once said, a thought cannot be unsaid by any other means. Have you ever seen someone un-fart a fart?

OK, Sana, I know in my heart that I'm not like that.

Sana replied, recourse to the heart never works in logic.

No, I cried, I'm talking to a friend, the relationship is based on the heart, you may be able to read my disposition, which as you know is not chauvinistic. So let me continue with my tale.

So I was like that great circumlocutionist, always ended up not getting the women I loved... There was this girl, Finda; we grew up together. She was sweet and I really yearned her. But I just couldn't tell her so. A friend told her he wanted her and before I knew what was happening they were married. I was so bitter that I stopped yearning her. So now I was braver in my talks with her, freer, like when wooing women I didn't love.

When she gave birth, I visited her. 'Finda,' I said, 'do you know this child would've been mine?'

'I know, 'she replied, 'and I was waiting for it from you; desperately needed it from you, but you didn't come, so I paired up with Sorie.'

So you see, I was a coward with women I loved.

The only woman I really loved that I ever succeeded in getting was Naphat. I loved Naphat with all my soul, all my heart. But she was that very good girl and I sort of thought good girls don't take kindly to being wooed. So I didn't talk wooingly anytime we met. But one day it worked out for me, just like that. It was at a party and Bubu music was pumped at us. Bubu Music, O Bubu Music! Everybody went wild, and we danced off-guardedly. Naphat was gyrating her buttocks into my wriggling groins and I was flicking her nipples the way a religious fanatic flicks chaplet in a divine ecstasy... After the party I carried her home. That was how our love flowered, so unexpectedly. And so unexpectedly were the flowers of our love dunked. It started one December when one fat stoutly dressed heavenly jewelled holiday maker from America spotted her dancing with me in the dance floor of the popular Isabella Nightclub at the seafront of middle Romeron. He ogled her the way David ogled Bathsheba bathing the otherside of his garden walls. He sent his foot soldiers to get her and they came, t-shirts tightly hugging chests bouncing with huge 'threaten'- that's how we call big gaudy chains glittering with the loudness of fake-gold. Those chains could truly threaten you to submission. That is, if you are, as we say in Eastern Romeron, 'a dead.' But I'm not a dead, I'm wise in the ways of the fake. So I didn't allow them to cart away my Naphat to the holiday-maker. I mean this was not the 1940s when they had 'Gents Excuse'- a man wanting to dance with the damsel you are dancing with comes and pats your back and you let him dance with her.

But you know I must speak the truth because Naphat may one day read this autobiography of a die heard Eastern rarayboy who went to Hilltop College and raise such a hell as to make people think it's all fiction. I know her; she will do it if I don't put the records straight.

So I speak the truth:

It was really Naphat's will rather than mine that stopped the footsoldiers. She was not Bathsheba and our holidaymaker was not David, or so I thought. Pressure, do you know what pressure is? Peer pressure family pressure? A friend of Naphat had struck it gold with a holidaymaker and she was now in America and Naphat's other friends told her after reminding her of this, 'babe this is your chance to strike the American gold.' And her family too, the holiday maker went there giving money to one day old babies and hundred years old grannies and all other ages in-between. And these said, 'Naphat do you not want to make it in life, must you stick to a poor good for nothing who may leave you if he strikes gold.'

And they reminded her of a cousin of hers. This cousin loved this guy called Modu, and Modu was yet at college, and cousin was a hard selling market woman, and she sponsored her love through college, and through his unemployment days after college. And then Modu struck gold. And he ditched cousin, and he married a woman who had once ditched him but came flying to him when he struck gold, or should I say diamond, that he struck diamond, for ours is also a land of diamond at Kono, Boajibu and other places. I once went to Boajibu. I was then at Hilltop college. I decided to go there to a cousin to, as we say, 'dreg.' I came back with money, cash that any student would be proud of.

So cousin, I mean Naphat's cousin, was ditched for this other woman. Pressure on Naphat; even from

122

this cousin, 'I've seen it,' she told Naphat, 'don't rely on love in making your choices; it only leads to betrayal, betrayal.' (Now don't try to get at my story by asking how I got to know about what cousin told Naphat. Answer: I pieced it up, creatively, by reading between behavior).

Naphat collapsed under her cousin's account. It was an account of real experience; one, as we say, of a person who not only saw it with its own eyes, but also held it with her own hands, and it scorched her, scorched her to the very soul. The guy who did it to cousin is now safely in some palace with his wife, enjoying every bit of it.

'Don't you think those who do evil necessarily pay for it,' Cousin Duramani or Brother Duramani or... told me months ago. 'Saying one who does evil gets evil later is nothing but a myth... The world moves on, most people got away with it, with what they did, no retribution. But simpletons still believe in people getting evil for evil... you see this thinking everywhere. You go to churches or mosques and there's this Preacher saying a suffering man or nation is paying for some evil deed; or that an evil person will surely pay for it, and this Preacher will tell stories of past evil men paying for it, like Pharaoh like Judas, like Abu Jahl, like Pol Pot, like like like, and where these evil men did not pay for it, they say they will surely pay in times to come, they shall be raised and punished... These stories irritate me... Or you go to a theatre, and you see the play being artificially bent to make someone pay for what he or she did. Or you read a novel and you see this same wishful thinking... an eye for an eye, a heart for a heart... Mate, don't allow that nonsense to weaken your resolve to prevent being hurt now... Don't rely on hurt being paid by hurt, resist being hurt...'

These thoughts resuscitated me; I must not allow this anguish to continue. So I dashed home, to tell this woman visitor that I loved her, wanted her; and more than that: tell dispenser- friend to mouth-off her... I met dispenser-friend's mouth off hers. She had been resuscitated; and she was sitting at the far end of the bed, back against wall, shanks crossed, heels touching shins, just the way practiced Sheikhs sit at mosques. She jerked when she saw me, and outstretched arms, like one about to fly. She smiled, I smiled back. She changed her sitting posture: right insteps against left heel, left calf almost touching back of left thigh; head resting on left knee-cap; hands crossed about left ankle, right fore-finger on right bit toe. I sat near her. I hugged her. I kissed her. I whispered into her ears, 'I love you.'

'Me too,' she replied.

Dispenser-friend was gawping at us. I said to him, 'excuse us for a while.'

'No,' my woman-visitor shouted, 'he saved my life.'

'So you want him around?'

'Yes, I love him too.'

'To hell with him,' I shouted. I was annoyed, angrier than Jesus at the temple-capitalist. (You see sometimes I'm inclined to believe those writers who argue that all male-fights, wars, raids, etcetera, are battles for women bodies or spaces considered feminine – land, farms, country, etcetera)

'No,' yelled woman-visitor

'This is my room, I decide who stays here.'

'No' she thundered again.

'I'll go' dispenser-friend said.

'I'll go with you,' woman-visitor told him.

'No,' he replied, 'stay with him.'

The woman was now transfixed between dispenser-friend or rival and I. Here she was being snubbed by a man I considered a 'dead', a bumpkin. I loved her, but now she seemed ordinary, she could be jilted, denied, not desired. The goddess was dethroned and heaven did not give a damn.

Who told you anyone needs a particular person? Asked Cousin Duramani or... No particular person is indispensable to anybody's life. Love is a genetically ingrained fiction to force us to be social. Love is a particularizing of sociability. But the particular person could be dispensed with. For it is written, here, here, now, now: the particularizing of love is the beginning of slavery.

I laughed, a long one, a liberating understanding was bobbling within... I would go about the world, unconcernedly, telling all I love them. I won't fear the consequences, if they refuse me, they too can be refused, they are humans, ordinary humans... oh no I would never again see a loved one as somehow superhuman...o no.

Dispenser-friend hissed and walked away. I thought aloud, 'I'm going.' Woman-visitor or lover thought I was speaking to her, 'No don't go.'

'I'm not speaking to you,' I thundered and dashed out.

QUANTUM NONESENSE: NEITHER HERE NOR THERE; THE SAME THING IS BOTH NEW AND OLD

I slithered through the slough of our reality and entered the leaning house of Sana. The slithering peeled away my confidence and I entered Sana's leaning miracle of Pizza confused.

'Sana,' I called out 'I am confused, distraught.'

'It won't last,' Sana replied, 'confusion is but a disequilibrium between our reminisces and dreams, but the confusion may soon end and your equilibrium restored. Though that too may be fleeting'

This did not make sense to me, 'Sana, I don't understand.'

Sana explained, 'the human being means you, fleeting means that which ends soon, equilibrium means balance, reminiscing is dreaming about the past, dreaming is remembering the future.'

I was still confused, 'Sana, you are a bad dictionary I asked you to explain a phrase and you come up with a more difficult one.'

'Many many years to come all those people you are meeting now will gather in some corner of the universe trying to remember what is happening now.'

127

'You confuse me Sana.'

'All the dreams and happenings that constitute
you had once happened to other persons long before
you were born.'

How come?' I asked.

'Do you believe that you are the only person
in the whole of history that had met a woman at the
gates of a cemetery?'

'No.'

'Do you want to tell me that you are the only
bereaved person   in the whole of history that had
dreamt about winning the love of a displaced woman?'

'No.'

'Do you want to tell me that you are the only lover
in the whole of history that had had a nightmare about a
friend wanting to take his love from him?'

'No.'

'So you see all these events had happened
before. That is why the good book says there is nothing
new under the sun. But I   say unto you, never before
had all these events combined to happen to an individual

the way they combined to happen to you. You are the only point in space-time in which all these things happened the way they did. Many many years to come, beings will gather in some place in the universe trying to remember all what happened in your space-time point. You are that remembering, you are that dream, you are that point'

'Me a point?'

'Yes, viewed from the vastness of time and space you're a very little skein of dreams and reminisces....'

I shouted, 'what about when viewed by myself.'

Sana was a little taken aback, 'perhaps, then you're more than a point, less or more of a dream or reminisce... You become consciousness, sub-consciousness, unconsciousness; a logic and illogic going into one another... mingling and disintegrating into new tiny enriched or improvised bits that float wildly or go into another fleeting equilibrium... or disequilibria... Which do you prefer to call yourself?'

Sana pushed his mad head forward, almost butting me. I flinched back, 'none.'

'Why?' Sana asked.

'Who does the remembering when nothing lasts?' I asked.

'Spirits, shadows, empty casks devoid of what constitute them, hollow   beings   trying   hard   to   remember contents.'

'I don't understand.' I said

'You've seen snails? Sana asked.

'Of course yes,' I replied

'The shell of the snail covers what the snail is made up of. The shell protects the insides.
But the snail has one great weakness –it is very slow, and this was making it a harder job for the shell to protect the snail. An argument ensued. The shell accused the insides of slowing down their common existence. The insides accused the shell that the slowness was caused by the shell. The argument got nasty. The solution became the separation of the shell and the insides. The insides could not withstand the exposure, so it rotted. The shell was free of the inside but it lost purpose. It was tossed about everywhere. That is us, we are shell-beings without contents, we are faster now in taking decisions, in moving about, in doing just about everything. But we are either reminiscing about our lost contents or dreaming about new ones. We miss our contents.'

'I do not understand,' I said.

'You're tragically stupid.' Sana replied.

130

'Perhaps.' I replied

'You're a very awkward fellow.'

'I've been told that before.'

'By who, when, where?'

'At Hilltop College, by a lady called, O The-God/ess I just can't remember her real name. I have turned the whole encounter into a short story.'

'Well, good, read me the short story.'

'I call her Maimuna in the story, and call myself Sana Tana.'

'Why should you change your name?'

'Changing my name creates a little distance between me and the story, and I think a little distance makes me tell it a little more clearly; it gives one's leeway to play with the facts.'

'But why change it to my name?'

'Using the name of people you know in fiction makes it a little more real.'

OK, OK, read me the story.'

Sana Tana stared at the plate of rice and cassava leaves sauce, then at the fork and knife. 'How do they expect me to eat with this,' he murmured.'

Just then a waiter, a stout one with a physique that would remind one of an upright frog passed along. '...Em em sir, can I use my hands,' Sana Tana blurted.

'No, this is college,' the waited replied, 'a civilize place, eating with hands is forbidden.'

'Sir, I'll wash my hands after eating.'

'There is no water or towel for that,' the cousin to the frog croaked.

Sana Tana felt the heavy weight of eyes all over him. 'God help me escape this disgrace...'

He had scarcely finished this prayer when in a desperate act of faith in its efficacy he grasped the knife with his right hand and tried to shove the rice to the fork on his left hand.... No, his movement were awkward; he missed his target and splashed the cassava leaves sauce on his immaculate shirt.

Someone quaffed; a frightening sense of imminent disgrace flooded Sana Tana. He shivered, loosening his grip on the fork, which - no, he tried to catch it, letting go the knife, which somersaulted thrice before joining the fork in a clanging protest on the dirty floor of the dining hall.

God! God! God! Sana Tana was drowning in a boisterous laughter of civilization... Wicked soul, no one amongst these civilize diners came to his rescue. None.

Except Maimuna.

She tugged Sana Tana unto the buoyancy of her beautiful being and rowed him to a quieter place.

'Look,' she told him, 'never panic, even when you don't know what to do. Be ignorant confidently. They would think you are stylish.'

Sana Tana felt a warm smile on his scalp and raised his bowed head - what a beauty... a dark luminance, nose as - Sana Tana ran out of resolve and looked away.

'I'm Maimuna,' she smiled as she joined Sana Tana on the grass.

'Sana Tana,' he gasped.

'Sana Tana,' said Maimuna, 'innovation is nothing but confident awkwardness that somehow eases the inconvenience of this heavy artifice of civilization we must have in order to survive in this exilic condition... You hear, to stay put, don't panic when an additional burden of civilization is added unto you... You know about gravitation eh?'

'Yes,' Sana Tana stutters, 'I've read about it'

133

'Fine, your understanding is adequate to what I want to say.... Ours is a generation in the moon, in lunar time, weightless...if we don't have enough of these heavy hypocrisies around our beings, we shall not be able to hoist our identity.'

'I don't understand.'

'Without these norms of civilization, you would fly off to the weightless non identity of harrowing reminisces in a void of hopelessness...'

Sana Tana was confused; Maimuna was trembling with celestial revelations. Her hands were upwards, her décolleté radiant with the divine.
'....Or more frightening you could be pulled towards the gravitational intensity of Eden-earth where you would be blind and deaf to the snake-talk of copulation under trees with juicy but forbidden eye-opening fruits'.

'I prefer that,' Sana Tana finally found his voice, '....and with you.'

'No No No, no one could revert to that Eden innocence...the blazing sharp swords of the angels of memory guard against it. They will hack you into pieces, and you will end up in the gasping spheres around earth; pulled one end by fantasies of innocence, pulled the other end by the desirous experience of seeing and knowing and really feeling the beauty, the joys and the fulfillment of your now public parts.

End of story'

Sana yelled, 'that's not a good story.'

'What is a good story?'

'It is one that has a beginning, a middle, and an end. But your story does not have a beginning, a middle and an end. It does not have, if I should extend Maimuna's metaphor, the artifice of civilization they want us to put on to stay put in this lunar art of ours. Stories must have a beginning, a middle or an end, else they fly off to a freedom none could understand; a story must have a beginning, a middle or an end, else the storyteller becomes as mad as I am now.'

'You're making the ideas in my story mean more things than I meant.'

'Who told you it is your story? Once a story is out of you it is no longer yours? It now belongs to those who listen to it or read it. Come to think of it, even in its creation it was not yours, for your materials were stolen from encounters. Stories are but recounting of encounters; they are but bridging of episodes hitherto separated by many other episodes.'

'What if one lacks materials to make the bridging?'

'Well then stuff in your stupidity, your dreams, your fears, your other memories.'

Okay Okay, let me continue the story of Sana Tana and his fork and knife:

So it was that Sana Tana got used to eating with a fork and knife; so it was that Sana Tana felt so proud that he stole a fork and knife from the college dining hall; for sure back home he would impress with this new civilize habit.

So it was that when he was called by his slum peers to the common peer bowl he took out the knife and fork. This surprised his companions.

'Why won't you eat with your palm?' 'Palm Oil dirties the hands of he who writes on papers, soils it.'

Some so marvel at his deftness with the fork and knife that they stared without eating.
Others ate but got their fingers bruised and cut, the pepper in the food burning them to their very souls.

So it was that eating with Sana Tana became very dangerous. So it was that Sana Tana started eating alone.

So it was that others so marvel at him for daring this that they composed a song for him during watch night.

So it was that Sana Tana became so ensconced in this that he forgot how to eat with others.
Especially now that he has these flat plates that bare hands could not eat in... Not even two people with knives and forks could

for the prongs would go into each other and some of the food would fall on the floor which is very indecent.

Especially now that Sana Tana has somehow acquired some white colored carpet for his dining room... Even for his toilet which because his mother still has those old toilet habits, she has been banned from using.

'Good, good good!' Sana jumped, almost butting the sky, 'you stuffing in your stupidity, dreams, memory, your story is becoming a very good one'

I was confused by Sana's sudden enthusiasm for my unconventional story. I asked him, 'even where it does not have a beginning, middle and an end.'

'Those artifices are sometimes good, but need they bind you always? Come to think about it, the artifices are not part of you. Even where they are part of you, they can be excised when they become unbearable?'

'You are a mutilator.'

'Listen, beloved, the imagination sometimes works like the bio-engineer. Just as the bio-engineer splices and rejoins cells hitherto separated by thousands of cells, so also your imagination splices and rejoins episodes hitherto separated by thousands of intervening events.'

The Preacher warned us against joining things that should not be joined. Nothing, in itself, is evil. What is

137

evil is putting asunder what the Lord has joined and joining what the lord has sundered. Guard your imagination; else it blows your being into smithereens. Guard your imagination; else you fall into the void of insatiability. Guard your imagination; else you become a munafiqun, a heckler, one that is afraid to take sides. Guard your imagination, else you become an indecision, the worse type of being; worse than the unbeliever. For the unbeliever can be placed, can be seen. But the heckler creates confusion; he is a maker of mischief.'

'No,' I told Sana 'I don't want to be a heckler. I must do the instinctual; I must tell my woman visitor about all the corners of my soul.'

DEATH AND RESSURRECTION

So I rushed home, kicking my room door. 'Woman woman,' I gasped. She was not around. I darted under-bed. Turned the bed upside down.Turned over the suitcases.Brought down shelves. Tore ceilings. 'Woman woman...'

Then the thought gripped me, and coldness snaked around my loins, and my thing shriveled, like when taking bath in Harmattan morning ...Is not this woman visitor the most talked about Yellow Woman? She moves along, this Yellow vampire, in a guise and gait magnetic to her prey. You woo her, carry her home and just as... Noooo, woman visitor or lover couldn't be her... But I didn't know her name... I didn't know the name of woman-visitor, the name name... O yes a ghost a ghost...

'Ghost, ghost, ghost,' I yelled.

Relatives came running, 'what ghost, your father?'

'No, no, no,' froth filled my mouth. I passed out...

I woke up in some nether world. And there was my woman visitor, fetus coiled, near a garbage can, flies were her friends. And as I sat down, these buzzed the stench of my trepidation, 'what do you want near me, what?' she screamed.

'I love you...'

She was vexed the more, 'do you know my name?'

'How can I know your name when you haven't told me?'

'You never allowed me, I'm an aborted being, forced out of my cozy world by men with iron extensions...tell me, do fetuses have names?'

This got me mulling over names. The names the names, and Adam-Hawa, also called Adam- Eve was taught the names. And The-God/ess assembled the celestial beings. 'Tell me the names.' But they couldn't. But Adam-Hawa told the names and The-God/ess commanded the celestial beings to bow before Adam-Hawa. All bowed except Iblisa also called Satan. He was rebellious, one of the disbelievers.

The names the names, and Juliet said, 'what's in a name O Romeo, change it...'
The names the names, and a rose by any other name will smell as sweet...

The name the names, and James Ngugi, decolonizing the mind, became Ngugi wa Thiongo.

The names the names, and many African-American became X's cutting the shackle-hold of slave-names.

140

So Malcolm Little became Detroit Red, then Malcolm X, then El Hadj Malik el Shabbaz

The naaames the names, but somehow Adam-Hawa did not tell their own very names, so The-God/ess kicked himher out of the Garden of Evenings to live in earthly ignorance of themselves. Hawa, which in English means desire, was dropped in the east; Adam, which in English means earth, was dropped in the west. The world was one big super-continent called Pangaea.

Desire at the farthest end, Earth at the other, the search for themselves began...
They had pictures of each other in the mind. They dreamt meeting each other, embracing, bursting the blisters in each other's soles; the nodules on the skin... each woke up with the other's pus inside hisher finger-nails...

They imagined; the imagination gave each vistas of the other's location, but limbs were weak, they woke to their recumbent loneliness, far apart; each went to a cave of dreams, dinosaurs roaring...

In their dreams he knew her. And she begot twins, a girl and a boy.

And the boy strayed.

And a birdlike creature, like Sinbad's, found him. It was the mythical dinosaur, the most successful being

141

then, very intelligent. It remembered seeing a new being like this boy the otherside of Pangaea and carried him to him.

And Adam and Hawa dreamt again. And he knew her. And she begat another set of twins, a boy and a girl. And the boy strayed and fell into a river and a fish, a mythical one, much like   Jonah's, swallowed   and vomited   him on   the   land   of   his   father...

A community of males; a community of females.

And the little males and females started dreaming each other. And behold, the first twin-girl was so beautiful. And the two brothers disputed as to who should know her in his dream. And their father told them to lay their disputes before The-God/ess. And before The-God/ess each presented a sacrifice. One brother presented some vegetables; the other brother killed an animal, blood was in his hands, red steaming blood. And The-God/ess was pleased with the one who killed and judged in his favor...

And the other brother reasoned thus: If The-God/ess could decide in favor of one who killed an animal, Hesheit would surely be happier with one who gives a more precious blood, and what blood is more precious than that of a brother?

So this brother led his brother to a lonely field; and made him, in the manner of a game they used to play, turn the

142

other cheek and look yonder. Then he took a dagger, the same with which his brother slew the animal, and in the self same way struck his brother's nape.

And brother that had been struck turned, and behold, there was a vista of his father and he yowled, 'father.'

But the vista drew a machete and cut him down, much like that bad father of a ritual murderer his child. And blood rushed out, as if it wanted to ask whether it was father that so unkindly stabbed, much like Caesar's blood Brutus.

But it was not father that struck. For father was at that very moment in a trance; the air cool, birdsong slow and apples glow in the low sun-flow... The snakes within are aroused... Eve's not a woman but this time as sneaking whisperer unto the breasts of menwomen to nibble nipples in the gloaming.

Evenings when shadows of all things merge, what lonesome mud-soul, also called earth-desire, wouldn't cover nakedness with fallen shade, also called leaves, which since they are now fallen should be called under-leaves to distinguish them from the top-leaves still hanging on trees...

The-God/ess' dazzling toe-nail is rustling the under-leaves.

And both Adam and Hawa also called Eve cried to each other, 'Gosh, there's the overstayed light gives distinction

143

to merging shadows; come, quick, hide your nudity in mine.'

'Who told you you are naked?' asked the Light

'Your light, the muezzin's call to dawn prayer.'

...Said the muezzin of our area, 'leave your spouses; prayer is better   than   your spouses... O ye who believe, when tempted   again, say I seek refuge in the Lord who splits darkness with light...'

Ah, so you don't know about muezzins? Let me tell you: they the loudspeakers of our faith, bellowers of the word made into gold-earrings for the ears of believers. The first one was called Bilal the Ethiop, the freed slave, his prayer-call was the earliest of Negro spirituals: 'join the chariot of prayer, join the chariot to success, there is no The-God/ess but the The- God/ess of Abraham, Ishmael and Muhammad.'

Anyway, let me continue the tale of names and the travails of Adam and Hawa. And Adam and Hawa also called Eve juddered in their hypnotic remembrance of things past: their separations, expulsion, their unending search for each other, for that unity in the under-leaves that the light sundered.

Behold! In their lonely shivering they dreamt themselves building a tower to stall their scatteredness. And they called the tower Babel, also called Babila, now called

Babylon, the Rastas' name for the West, though, of course that place was in the East.

Of course, said Younger Brother, they know it was in the East; they are using it to symbolize the arrogance of the West

Okay Younger Brother. And the tower they built to stall their scatteredness was so arrogant that it reached the skies.

And just as they were about to seal their achievement the Light created chasms and the tower fell. Pangaea was no longer one huge landmass, volcanic Light created chasms, lands drifted apart, continents emerged, mud drifted apart, The-God/essbreath couldn't hold the mud particles, brother/sisters red red blood was loosed upon the earth. Especially on the Atlantic, the slave routes to the Americas; particularly on the Indian Ocean, to Arabia and Persia. And sisters blood too, rape upon rape, like during the war in Salone, like even before the war in Salone, as in this story told us by a cousin-in-law:

Whilst in secondary school, a boarding school, some government notables visited a town not far away. Our principal chose six of us to help out with the welcoming ceremony. We did our best, getting food here, smiling there and answering questions about school and dreams over there.

I met my friend, Sata there. She had also been chosen by her school. She was a nice girl, very intelligent, but reserved...very very reserved.

Unlike me. I was everywhere at once, here, there, down there. It was a really exhilarating moment, cute girls being showered with admiration by the crème de la crème.

But as night fell, Sata became restless; she said she wanted to return to school. Soon her contagion caught hold of us. The place was getting very dark, the crowd was dispersing. Sata was now crying. We wanted to return to school, to our nightly talk of our daily exploits.

That was not to happen. Our principal burst upon us announcing, 'Girls, the buses that should have taken you back to school have some problems, but don't worry, the principal of Masama is making arrangements about getting you lodged at the Government Guest House.'
The Government Guest House! The talk of the region! More thrilling exploits to talk about at school.

Beloved, beloved, I wish we had kicked the principal and walked to school. Beloved Beloved, it was a trap, a heinous snare. The notables, men as old as our fathers, raped us. They raped me in the same room they raped Sata. I fought back, kicked, pinched, howled. But Sata didn't, she was too stunned, men as old as our fathers raping us. The only thing that would make you know Sata didn't like what they were doing to her were the tears rolling down her cheeks...'

And woman's burden is remembrance of things past. The snake of man spat its venom into her womb before it collapsed; the issue is this Cain also called Kabila who killed his brother to rape his sister...

146

like during the war in Salone. Like the invasion of Freetown, January Six Nineteen Ninety Nine. Freetown, also called Fritong, formertimes called Romeron, the wailing places, by those who, self referentially, are ancient, Themne. Romeron, land of vertical streams and mountain lashing waves, and thunder, and ancient wailing that frightened a drunken Portuguese into calling the place Sierra Lyoa, lion mountains, mountains of roaring lions. Freetown, place of mountains re- echoing wailing on the death by steep-stream drowning of a community being, wuni ki payt, being of a settlement, the name for the human being in the language of the Themne.

And man's burden is remembrance of things past; he carries the corpse of his murdered brother. How should he dispose of it? He carries this image of his act, wherever he wanders. The rot drips on him, maggots mixing in his soul. What can't he just fling this guilt and march on free; can't he cast off this burden?

And father died, calves stung by snakes within, mud-lust swallowed him whole.

'We're going,' I heard an aged voice amidst the wailing, 'anyone who has to pay Momodu should say it now or report to his family. Like-wise his debtors. All debts must be settled here, in this world. Next world things will be different, an unpaid one cent debt shall be heavier to tote that an elephant...

147

'Hear O hear, you youths who say 'I'm still young, still have time to reconcile with The-God/ess;;' here's Momodu, death struck him in the prime of youth...'

Me? Dead? Perhaps, they say corpses could hear but are unable to reply, to get up; am I a corpse?

'Death claims all,' I heard the preacher continue, 'even The-God/ess's friend. There was Anabi-Brima, the friend of The-God/ess. When the Angel of Death wanted to claim his life he cried to The-God/ess-on-high, 'O The-God/ess my friend, how can you kill your friend?' The-God/ess replied, 'O Anabi-Brima my friend, how can a friend be afraid to meet a friend?

'Nothing changes one's time to die, why then must you fear these ordinary mortals who threaten you with death to keep you under their evil designs. The Tanzil says 'Do not think that they that die in the way of The-God/ess are dead,' They're not, they rest in The-God/ess bliss, and in the hearts and prayers of the best among living mortals. That's what we should do, remember Momodu in our prayers, perchance the Deity on High would lesson the burden of his sins.

'Nothing changes the place where one is to die. There was this rich man who the Angel of Death met and told that his time is nearly up. The rich man ordered his horsemen to run with him to the farthest corners of the earth. Behold he met the angel there; and the angel told him, 'rich man, this was where the earth to create you

148

was taken, and so here is where your debt of dust will be returned.' Momodu's earth was taken from Romeron, so here must it be returned.'

Me? Dead? I protested, rising with my shroud, 'no, I'm not dead, I'm not dead...'

People scattered, fright-assisted legs breaking Olympic records. The assertion of my flesh and blood existence continued, desperately now, for I had remembered what The Preacher once said: 'the soonest those who bury you start returning you'll rise up and yell for them not to leave you. But they will go for they can't hear you, you've become a phantom...'

Me? Now a phantom? No. I bit my hand, ferociously, blood gushed out. I held up the hand, 'I'm not dead, see, flesh and blood, blood'. Jesus said something like that to an assembled skepticism, 'see, see the nail marks. 'See see,' I shouted, 'see the teeth marks; see I'm not talking through the nose... I'm not yet dead, I'm a living man not a ghost I'm a living man...'

A woman's voice was the first to acknowledge my un-ghostly existence, 'Yea yea he's alive, amen, he is alive forever he is alive amen.' The woman, arms outstretched, was trying to rally them to her faith; but their fright assisted flight knocked her down. So she turned to me; it was my woman visitor, and she was saying, 'I yelled your existence but they held me tight, ah so tight, like hawk a chick, like hang man's noose round neck of unjustly condemned man, like rapist overpowering a woman's hands and feet... But your resurrection frightened their grasps off... O my OOO...'

We hugged, body-fronts touched, so tight, like Siamese twins, we will rather die in Singapore than get separated. No, that metaphor is insensitive to the memory of the brave Siamese Persian sisters who wanted to be separated in Singapore. My metaphor is stupid, utter nonsense. So I let me change it: we hugged, body-fronts touched, so tight, like the way the two lopes of kola-nut hug each other... Good, that metaphor sounds real African.

I am an African dribbling English words, beating nouns, scoring verbs. The English referee stares at the metaphors without bounds, could not see my sleight of hand, the Maradona like goal. Roger Milla, Pele, Okocha. Is football not an English game? The empire strikes back, reverse colonialism, African accents on a frown colony of English words, making the words tote meanings they were not created for, we are the slave drivers of English words, all hail Governor Soyinka, Conquistador, devotee of the forge, servant of Ogun, smelter of English words.

'What's your name, dear?' I asked woman visitor.

'Hawa,' she replied, 'and henceforth you shall be Adam, Baimbadama.'

The mourners returned; index fingers and thumbs at opposite end of gaping lips, tongues in surprise lolling, 'So Momodu you're not dead.'

'Call me Momodu no more; I'm Adam, Baimbadama and this woman here is Hawa. Until saved by Desire I was Earth. But now Earth is desirous, Earth is alive. Preacher-man, I'm this woman's husband. Preacher, bless my new name and marriage to Hawa...'

So it was that my funeral became my wedding and naming ceremony, a day of sorrow became a day of feasting. May The Deity bless Jimmy Cliff for that song: people felt like fishes out of water; now they were wondering what's the matter, for they used to look down on the corpse down below, they never thought I would be up there again.

'A few questions before I solemnize this marriage,' said The Preacher. 'Hawa, do you accept his calabash?'

'I accept his calabash, but if he comes with another woman, I'll break it. For I am a no-three-nights woman

'I accept his Kola, but if he comes with another, I'll spit it at his face, for I am a no three-nights-woman

151

'I accept his needles, his thread, I'll sew his torn things, but if he comes with another, I'll pierce his eyes with them, for I am a no three-nights-woman

'I accept his bitter Kola, things could be bitter sometimes, but if it gets as bitter as another woman, I'll pour bitterness down his soul for evermore, for I am a no three-nights-woman

'I accept his raffia fan, I will blow his hot rice cold, but if he comes with another, I'll fling the hotness at his head, for I am a no three-nights-woman

'I am no virgin, but I accept his white cloth, but if he wants my blood on it as a sign of my innocence, I'll give him menstrual blood as sign of my maturity, for I am a no-three- nights woman.'
'Do you accept her conditions?' asked The Preacher

'Yes I do.'

'Then you are by The-God/ess obliged to fulfil them. I now declare you wife and man'

Wife, wife, wife! I married my wife forty years before I was born. My wife herself told me the story. 'Ten years after our marriage I gave birth to your mother. Thirty years later, your mother gave birth to you. I was there when you were circumcised. I instructed the circumciser to give my husband a cute penis cut.' She was my first wife, that woman, my grand mother. Later I heard some funny good-for-something rascally sociologists call it fictive relationship.

Fictive relationships? Sometimes they get too real. There was this man who lived in the same compound with this other family. The other family had a young girl, barely ten. The man joked that she was his wife. And he would buy things for this little girl. One day the man came home with his girlfriend. This little girl was so incensed, so jealous that she took some hot boiling water from her mother's cooking place and threw it at the man's girlfriend. You get it, the line between the real and the fictive could be so blurred, so fuzzy. You just ask the girl friends of that fictive husband. A succession of them was harassed by this little girl. Some she threw piss at, others she cursed, some others she jeered at. She drove them all off until the man decided to quit his thriving girl friend business. That little girl grew up into a beautiful woman, went to university and well, left this fictive husband for a real husband. But the fictive husband would have none of it. 'What? After driving off all those women away from me you want to leave me? No way.' He cried his hearts out; the little girl turned beautiful woman would not budge. He offered to launder her menstruation knickers; the little girl turned beautiful woman would not budge. He called the masters of religion to beg her; the little girl turned beautiful woman would not budge. He implored the sisters of mercy to talk to her; the little girl turned beautiful woman would not budge. When news of the rebellion hit this fictive husband, he went off and joined the rebels; came back and shot dead the little girl turned beautiful woman.

Anyway let me leave that history of my first marriage and fictive marriages and concentrate on this one now between Hawa and I.

After The Preacher had declared us wife and man, a Jahil shouted, 'Rubbish, no man will accept that as a condition.'

'What he's accepted is lawful,' said The Preacher.

And The Preacher also said, 'Adam with Hawa also called Eve did sin but they learnt words of inspiration from their lord. 'Our Lord, we have wronged ourselves, if you do not forgive us, and have mercy on us, we will be among those who perish.' Then he turned to Hawa and I, 'Adam and Hawa, pray like wise!'

And we did pray.

But I didn't pray solemnly; too many stories; too many distractions. I was remembering the story about that man who dreamt having lots of money. But when he woke up he found nothing... 'Eee The-God/ess!' he exclaimed, 'why must you taunt my expectations?' And he, in the secrecy of his heart, planned revenge. Very early the next morning he washed, performed ablution, spread prayer-mat on floor, removed slippers, raised his hands to say the takbir the beginning of Muslim prayers. But mid air hands stopped, came down again to fold mat, 'look at The- God/ess,' the man said 'Hesheit will be sitting there now expecting me to pray to Himherit...none for you...'

'Prayers,' said The Preacher, 'who said The-God/ess needs our prayers. Look, our praises are imperfect; words are poor carriers of the real. The Tanzil says that even if all the trees were pens, all the oceans ink, they wouldn't be enough to write down the praises of The-God/ess. So praising The- God/ess is really for our own good; for that's our mission here, the only way to assert our existence. Says The-God/ess in the Tanzil, 'I didn't create manwoman and djinns save to worship me.' So you see worshipping The-God/ess is self realization.'

'Preacher,' I once confessed, 'I couldn't steady my mind during prayers... too much imagining of other things during prayers.'

'Satan,' he said, 'unshaped stories for stories sake are the handiwork of Satan. So anytime you start imagining whilst praying say, 'I seek refuge in The-God/ess from Satan the ever stoned one.' Anabi-Brima once said that stoning-of- Satan when that ever stoned one whispered unto him not to slaughter his son, Sumaila. Then Hajara also said it; then Sumaila also called Ishmail. Three stonings did that ever-stoned one got before he retreated.

155

So anytime he whispers unto your heart, say the stonings three times – a-uudubillah, a- uudubillah, a-uudubillah. And three my son, also means plurality, so say it as many as the times the ever-stoned one comes.'

O yes, says The Preacher, that stoning is still done by Muslims during annual pilgrimage to Mecca; they stone Shaitan

O waw, says Salifu; why should that not be the way we stone adulterers? Erect some effigy of the adulterer and adulteress and stone them. Must we stone the flesh and blood adulterer; should it not be the image of the adulterer or adulteress rather than their flesh and blood? The symbolic is all over us, the symbolic too has a place in our scheme of things, but why are we so fixated on the literal.

Laughing during prayers...We once did it too loud, me and Younger Brother. It was the way that stranger-imam was intoning the verses, in spurts, in gaps...Our jaws swelled in spurts, in gasps, in unison with the prayerful spurts...We tried to stop laughter, eyes opened wide, widest to prevent a jaw- burst...

MEN WITH PROMISCUOUS LIPS

Anyway let me cut the story short and move to the consummation of my marriage with Hawa. Nobody held down her legs like we did to Thuma to get Duramani to soak her. Ours was a jolly good one, well almost. I must speak the truth because Hawa may one day read this autobiography of a raray man from Eastern Romeron who went to Hilltop College and raise such a hell as to make people think it's all   fiction. I know her; she will do it if I don't put the records straight.

So I speak the truth:

Hawa takes off her gown and allows her loose skirt also called lappa to drop. I see a brown leather rope of cowries and multi-colored beads just above her hips. 'Hawa, what is that?' I asked.

'I got it from the medicine man; it is to wade off that rebel   rapist in my dreams. He comes in the guise of my father to thrust his thing the size of a pestle into me. But I am ready for him now.'

Younger Brother laughed when I told him about Hawa's dream, 'but a dream is not real, she need not go to such   lengths to wade off dreams.'

Sana retorted, 'if she says the dream is real to her, it is real to her.'

157

'Look,' said Younger Brother, 'life is not that fictitious.'

Sana replied, 'Life is a fiction, The-God/ess dreaming.'

'Get The-God/ess out of this,' I said

'Sure,' Sana said, 'I don't believe hesheit is really in this... For you see, hesheit may not be fictitious, the dreamer is real; only the images and objects of the dream are fictitious...We are the objects of The-God/ess' dream...yes, even when we encounter The-God/ess in this dream, we relate to himherit as an object of the real God/ess' dream, a fiction like us.... The God/ess we encounter in the dream of the God/ess is not the real God/ess. But many do not know this... Do you know what causes death? Do you know why we die?'

'So Sana,' said Younger Brother, 'you are a lie, a fictitious being, an object in a dream?'

'You too are, we all are'

'I'm real, you see flesh, you see blood, lymph, voice like you... I'm not an invincible man....I'm real real real...'

'But shouting like that can't make you real, did Soyinka not say a tiger does not shout its tegritude?'

158

'But did Achebe not say a lizard would praise himself if no body did?'

'Take this from me, when The-God/ess turns in hisherit dreams, we shall all dissolve, evaporate into nothingness... not fiction, not real, just nothingness.'

'Do you really believe what you are saying?' asked Younger Brother

'Most of the time, yes.' Sana replied

'Most of the time...what does that mean...are you a patch work of beliefs?'

'Yes, and that's exactly what makes me a dream, a patch work held together by a dreamer...Do you want to make me real, eh Adam, do you want to tie me with your ropes of reality, ropes of time, of space, of perception, your ossification of fiction, concretization of thoughts, imagination.'

'You are mad.'

'I know. Remember, my cranium was cracked during the beggars protest.'

And because you know, you will never get sane.'

'I don't want to get sane... Sanity is slavery, extreme slavery... To be sane is to live a dull life.'

'Now, does your The-God/ess have nightmares?'

'Yes, when the objects of hisherit dream run berserk.'

'Become as frightening as you?'

'Now you are coming around to my point... Yes...but I'm not yet nightmarish, or else hesheit would have turned in hisherit sleep and blotted me out...like hesheit did to many persons before... Many generations before....Sodom and Gomorah, Steve Biko, Lumumba, Papa Doc, millions and millions of people.'

'I wish I too could blot you out of my dream... you frighten me.'

'You playing The-God/ess, that's one of the thing hesheit hates.'

'Hawa says anyone who makes love to her when she is wearing the cord will become impotent. That is what is keeping the spirit in her dreams away from her.'

'That's her story, you better believe.'

'So you think Hawa should not throw away that useless cord around her waist.?' Younger Brother asked.

'How can she throw away her dream? The cord is what holds her together; it is what holds together the part of her you call weird and the part of you call real.'

'That cord can't make me impotent.'

'You want to assure yourself that it is a lie eh, why this returning into it over and over again?'

'It's a lie.'

'You mean the opposite.'

'No way,' I shouted, 'I am not latching on to another meaning of the word. The Preacher once said, '...the word the word, the different meanings of the word, that's the source of unfaith. Those who have faith follow the established meaning of words; those without follow the metaphorical implications. That's Iblisa al-Garur also called Satan's trump card, he makes you imagine the thousands of metaphorical implication of every word; you now have variety, as the situation predisposes you jump from one meaning to another, you become untrustworthy, skeptical, without faith in anything, you become a heckler, a munafiq, and unbeliever. Is it for naught that the Kitabul-huda, the book of guidance, also called the Koran, which in English means the recitations, curses those who follow their dreams!'

Sana yelled, 'let priests in fiery sermons melt and the wide arch of ranged religions fall, I love the gorgeous

161

word, the word fully dressed, the word going to party.....the dancing word.'

Younger Brother was for a while as quiet as 2am, only to jump at Sana's ears like an alarm clock, 'I worship the lean word, the word stripped naked.... I hate flamboyance, so wasteful, confusing, corrupt. I worship the word laid bare, naked on the bed or where ever, ready to fuck, and be fucked, to procreate, to fill the world with useful thing. My soak had a nephew with a very big head...'

'Hydrocephalus,' I said

'Yes that's the condition,' Younger Brother continued, 'but the relatives said the boy was an evil spirit. So they neglected him, cursed him, despised him. My soak could not take that. She fed him, clothed him, gave him sweets. The relatives called her a witch on account of her kindness to her own nephew. Is there a belief weirder than that?'

'But that could have been another side,' said Sana, 'another equally true side of ...'

'No, Sana, no, the big head might have been a genetic defect exacerbated by delayed labor that led to an excessive remolding of the boy's cranium. His mother was a small woman, a little teenage girl, just like Duramani's wife Thuma.'

'Get Thuma out of this,' Duramani blurted.

'Resemblances, Duramani, resemblances, the little teenage girl was, just like Thuma, hoodwinked into marrying an old he-goat like you.'

'Don't get too hot,' Duramani told Younger Brother, 'I was only joking.'

'But this is a serious matter. The boy's mother died in labor... vagina hemorrhaging... Her cervix was small and the boy's head was so big that its thrust to get out peeled off the young woman's tender circumcision scar... Yes that's the truth, the naked truth... had we allowed that in to our heads, then our lot would have been much better.... But no....they hated the nude word, the naked truth; so they contrived all sorts of weird lies around their useless practices...weird lies... your gorgeous words, your dancing words.... Ambiguities, they abandoned the orphaned child, they said the child killed his mother... How could that be? So they tried to kill him by abandoning him under the cotton tree with sacrificial egg, palm oil, rice flour all around.'

'What became of him?' I asked.

'The relatives said he would disappear, become a snake and disappear. But no, my soak found him crying and kicking the air. She rescued him. But the relatives cursed her for bringing the poor little boy home.'

163

'So, he is still alive?'

'No, he was a torment to them, so they killed and fed him to mangy cats.'

'No, Younger Brother, that's a lie.'

'It's the truth, Bambadama, the whole truth.'

'Shut off your impudent tune,' said Duramani, 'that can't be the whole truth...You can't render the whole truth.... No one can render the whole truth about anything. There could have been more to that boy than meet your eyes.'

'What meets my ears is what I condemn. They neglected the boy, that's what I know and that's what I condemn.'

'Do you know me?' asked Duramani.

'Sure I know you, you are my blabbering cousin, the maker of meaning out of nothing.'

'I mean do you know all about me.....the stories that I consist of, my physiology, my psychology, my history my...'

'What are you trying to get at?'

'Nothing, only that we can't know the whole truth......the whole picture... only montages, flashes, half truths, inconclusive evidences.'

'And so?'

'We should be careful about passing judgment, about condemning, for the evidence is inconclusive.'

'So because we can't know all, we should not pass judgment on the little we know.'

'We should be careful... that's all...we should not talk and behave as if we know everything about everyone... half truths should not be the basis for total condemnation.'

'My soak's people neglected the boy for nothing... all else is superstition, lies as fanciful as the cord around Hawa's waist.'

'Get my woman's waist out of this,' I said.

'But you yourself puked the topic at them.' It was Hawa. I did not see her enter the place of our boys' talk. 'And now your mouth stinks with the after-slime of vomited words. O Man with lips that open up to any penis of an ear, man with promiscuous lips, were your lips not initiated into a secret society, must you tell your consummation of your marriage with me to the whole damned world... tell me tell me what use telling me to the world?'

'Fulfilling the prophecy of my father; he told my mother that I'll become a great tale teller; but frankly speaking I don't know,' I replied.

'Don't know?' She looked at me coldly, the coldness made me judder.

'Oh Hawa,' I blubbered, 'your eyes are cold.'

She ignored me and asked Younger Brother 'You hate my amulet eh?'

Younger Brother replied, 'it's a useless string of cowrie shells and fanciful beads. That's the truth, the whole truth about it. It has no other...'

Sana butted in, 'say you don't have eyes for them; you need perceptual aids, more experiences. Tell me man, can you see your microbes without a microscope, without the subtle molding to believe that what it presents corresponds to what they say are characteristics of living things. Come to think of it, all knowledge, all realities are acts of faith, faith in one's senses or in those things we say help our senses to see more, feel more, know more... Just lose faith in something and you see nothing but superstition... That's it, knowledge in reality is nothing but forceful faith in the concretization of thoughts about the nature of existence.'

Younger Brother replied, 'I have faith in that which works, that which produces results.'

'Me too,' Hawa, said, 'this amulet has produced results. It has authenticity for me... for my being as an individual of a unique circumstance.'

'There is nothing unique about your situation... you are just another woman, another superstitious woman.'

'You missed her point,' said Sana. 'Nothing like her has ever existed, and will never exist. She is a unique nexus of genes and circumstances. Her spatio-temporality is unique, there is only one her.'

'No way,' said Younger Brother, 'everything she has, other people have, other people have breasts, voice, hair and their occasional fits of wild weird beliefs.'

'Duramani is right,' Hawa shouted, 'I am a unique being. This is my breast, not another woman's breast, this is my waist, these are my hips. Yes, other women have breasts, brains, hips, beliefs, experiences, but the mix of these things in me is unique, no other one is the same as this mix of cells, blood and memories.'

Memories, memories, bubbling memories of deviance, deviant memories... Like that time, during my inkblot class six years when an older relative took Younger Brother and I to play the game of buttered behinds. The nasty criminal rubbed butter on our behinds and tried to shove his thing down. We hollered. The neighbors caught him and tethered his penis to a tree all day long. Worse than that, they sang his shame during watch night. It was such a beautiful song that people took to singing it every time every day. The shame drove him away, and we do not know to this moment where he is.

But Younger Brother loved the smell of butter on anus. Nights he would rub butter on backsides and sniff. I knew it was him, but since he didn't rub butter on my backside (of course the smell of my mat-wetting would over-smell a buttered backside) I would fake consternation mornings when victims of anal butter cried their embarrassment.

Memories memories, this one leads to that, memories lurking in wait, like armed-robbers, like rebels, to ambush the unsuspecting present. I put my hand to scratch my itching newly-shaven pubic area and my finger smell like something else... O yes, like a cousin-in-law's passion-bubbling privates. It was raining and twentyish cousin-in-law thigh- clasped my class five head into her nude groins...

She was bad, that cousin-in-law. Little as I was I knew she was not doing what should be done, for she was always telling us to make sure no one knew what she was making us do, else she would do some very bad things to us. The other time she held down the daughter about my age of a tenant in our house and told me to put my thing into her thing. First she opened her up and I saw something like little bits of ill-ground groundnuts inside the girl my age. 'Is that groundnut?' I asked cousin-in-law.

But was it me or Younger Brother that asked, in the remembering of things I often mistake Younger Brother for myself and vice versa. I sometimes mistake Duramani for Sana and Sana for Salifi and vice versa.

'O yes,' Cousin replied, 'lick it'.

And I or Younger Brother or Salifu or Sana did   lick but   it didn't   taste like groundnuts. 'It didn't taste like groundnuts,' I heard Younger Brother say.

THE MURDER OF YOUNGER BROTHER

Stories, stories, stories, said the metaphor-mad workshop coordinator of the creative writing workshop, 'the good story builds up the way your beautiful woman or handsome man builds up. You meet, say, this woman, and you love her eyes; but going on you found out you don't like her ear curves. So next time you meet a woman, you look at her ear lobes; but going on you found out that her nose is unsatisfactory; so now you don't only look at eyes and ears but also nose. But going on you found out you don't like her feet, the shape of her calves, the splayed toes; so now you look at her feet...'

Hawa is my beautiful woman; pain and face drew me to her. But her hair, breast, feet, everything fits my feel of the beautiful... save... save this big tummy now five months old...this tummy, this blot on Hawa's beauty, this blot caused by a rapist...

'Hawa,' I say, 'my beautiful woman Hawa, you shouldn't have a bastard tummy, this your swollen tummy disheartens me'.

'It's part of me now, an indelible part of me...my blood'.

'But mixed up with the dirty blood of a rapist, a rogue's blood, impure...'

170

'I wish I could extract that blood from it but I can't. And I don't want to destroy my blood for the sake of somebody's. No, I don't want to sacrifice my blood to a rotten blood. No, I want my daughter back, the child I was forced to leave in the mud is here in this tummy. I can't throw her out again.'

'But Hawa this your tummy is the culmination, a forceful presence of things that shouldn't have happened... If one must start again, the child must die...'

'Adam, tell me, are you the culmination of the right things? Are you, as you stand here a being of fair outcomes through and through? Tell me tell me!'

This sends me mulling months and months... Am I the culmination of what ought to be done in all times past? My mind traversed to my namesake Adam; what if he hadn't gone near the tree? What if he hadn't been separated from Hawa and then kicked to this place? What if Adam, in his search for Hawa hadn't cut his heals at Karbala, his blood gushing unto that mount where generations later his grandson Al-Hussein ibn Ali ibn Abi Talib ibn Abdul Muttalib of Banu Hashim would be slain in a slaying that shamed history? But what if that grandson's immediate grandfather, Al-amin ibn Abdullah ibn Abdul Muttalib hadn't been stoned out of Taif, what would have been the state of my religion? What if The-God/ess hadn't demanded manwoman flesh in the encounter with Abul anbiyya also called Abram of Ur?

What if manwoman hadn't, as Duramani said, demanded God/ess flesh? What if the prey in manwoman-eating God/ess hadn't become the predator in God/ess-flesh-eating manwoman?

'But all that is religious myth,' said Younger Brother.

Good, I replied, the original meaning of the word 'myth' is 'stories of the supernatural,' and that's what I have just told you. But let us use another line of telling the story: what about the mass- extinctions at the end-Permian period 250 million years ago? What would have happened to my evolution if it hadn't happened? But perhaps 250 million years is a far off time too far off. But what about the extinction of the giant lizards, the dinosaurs, 65 million years ago, had the dinosaurs been around, would my ape-like ancestors have emerged and evolved into this greatest of all predators?

'But all that might be science fiction,' said Younger Brother

Okay, but what if the Empire of Songhai in the Near Sahel hadn't defeated the Kings of Mali, scattering about some of the people that gave rise to me to meet some of my other ancestors? What if the Sultan of Morocco hadn't destroyed Songhai, ushering a period of scatteration in West Africa that is literally true of the Arabic word-base for our continent – Ifrikiya, a scattering and weakness that culminated in the European conquest of our part of the world? What if the Moors

172

hadn't been brutalized out of Spain by Queen Isabella and others who stole the wealth of Muslims and Jews; what if that Columbus, sponsored by the Moor-defeat induced wealth of Isabella hadn't blundered into the Americas? What if there had been no slave trade, no establishment of a Province of Freedom in Salone, no defeating of Thomas Peters and Bai Bureh, no establishment of British rule on the weal of Nyagua, no imposition of Madam Yoko on the people of Kpa Mende, no coup after Independence and other mishaps that ossified into the Salone of my birth-time?

'But that is generalized history,' I imagined Younger Brother stating.

Just shut off your impudent tunes. I yelled. What if Mother hadn't been forced to marry Papa? What if I hadn't diarrhea in my infancy? What if I hadn't mat-wet? What if... O no, it seems as if all events before my birth, the real, the mythical, the illusive, were a conspiracy to get me to this earth, to this time... What if rebels hadn't attacked Hawa's village? What if Papa hadn't died, would I have met my heart's desire at the gates of Necropolis?'

I rushed to hug the past for happening as it did... If it had not, I, the most wonderful thing that has happened to me, would not have come into being... OOO the nice things, the brutalities, the mishaps... OOO I'm a mixture, the legitimate, the not so legitimate and the illegitimate co-exist in me, the pure

173

and impure mixing, like this child about to be born...

'Congratulations Mr. Adam' says the nurse, 'Ms. Hawa has successfully given birth to a boy, a big healthy boy...'

Ah this is me; I'm this child I love it... and I'll call it Foreh, after Younger Brother who just died. Impatience, they say. Their salaries were not forth coming and he left his forest post to go for it at Brigade headquarters. A group of soldier-hating vigilantes met him on the way, cutlass raised. Frightened, he shot two. The others rushed at him, overpowered him, tied him up and slit his nape... I'll name this child for him... Hawa and I had agreed on this. If it is a girl she names it, if it is a boy I name it... I'll call it Foreh, for Younger Brother, yea...

'What's wrong sir?' it's the nurse.

'The child, the child, is it like me, is it like me?'

'Perhaps...' the nurse replied.

'Can I see it now?'

'Yes, Ms. Hawa wants to see you.'

Alone with Hawa and son, Hawa says, 'it's not my daughter, it's his son, he resembles the rapist he... look

Adam I want to start anew, you told me to, so now I'll strangle this bastard child.'

With that she clasps the throat of the child, the clasping of a strong one.

'Noooo, you are killing my Younger Brother' I yell, holding her arms, twisting them, fighting to weaken the hawk-claws- on-chicken-neck clasp...

The clasping continues, she my brother's neck, me her arms burrowing phalanges to humerus, then ulna. A creaking sound; it's her ulna and the child's mandible.

'The deed is done, she shouts. 'waaiii my arm my arm... waaaiii..'

And my mind traverses to that first waaaiii I heard at the gates of my father's burial and I say, 'I'm sorry dear ah so sorry...'

'The deed is done,' she says.

'Yes but your arm, your broken arm..'

She stares at me, then at the corpse of Younger Brother, at me again, 'the deed is done; it is done.'

'But but but... he did nothing wrong...'

'Did I do any wrong when they raped me, what did my daughter do? Look don't burden my now with what has been done.'

'We can't extract ourselves from our memories...'

'Aaaiii my arm my arm...'

'I'm sorry so sorry.'

The policeman arrested Hawa soon afterwards. Murder, he said. You killed your newly born baby. You have the right to remain silent or anything you say may be used as evidence against you in a court of ... you know the lines.

The child is a bastard, she replied. Bastards caused our war, those conceived in lawlessness, begotten in lovelessness, brought up in lordlessness.

O my O my, I cried, what a theory of war. But that is far better than that guy who said that the burning down of a college was to erase the facts that the rebels did not graduate; they burnt down the college to make the fact that they did not graduate as hard to see as cat's penis.

Or that other theory about the war as fighting for the rain forest. The apes are missing their forest, so they are killing each other for the little patches of it that remain. That is the sort of anthropological exotica that excites the Occident. I get it now O Sana, great friend, gatherer of the pricelss rubbish of the rich, librarian of the

176

dustbin, manwoman with the cracked cranium: *We are Jahiliyyans, people of ignorance, people ignored, relegated to the dustbins of remembrance; all the unwanted in people's remembrances are thrown at us; we are the replicas of their unwanted Darwinian beginnings – apes; we are replicas of their unwanted divine beginnings – Noah's Ham (Ham is pig made edible, useful. And also laughable, we are Ham actors, we do things badly); we are the spittoons for the phlegm of their souls.*

THE YOUTH OF PARADISE

At the gathering of roads I gather myself within, like skirts of women crossing a stream. This life's but a silent scream, rumbling quick like the holy mutterings between the two sermons of Friday noon prayers. I am muttering, quick, quick, God/ess, absolve us of this ugliness, let my beautiful woman go, may they not find her guilty of murdering that child, let my beautiful Hawa go

'Only beautiful birds are caged,' I hear Duramani echo, 'the ugly ones are let go.'

I replied, 'make her ugly then and free her.'

'You won't want her ugly; rather join the fight to make the beautiful ones free.'

I hired the best lawyers to get her free.

But Hawa queried, 'who told you to get lawyers, who told you I need intercessors?'

I replied, 'the contest is as uneven as wave marks on sandy shores.'

'Get out, get out,' she cried. 'The officers of the law must be lashing against the shoreline of your sanity. They are nightmares eating away your resolve.'

'That's why we need lawyers; mad guys like them that will drive them mad.'

'Me nor buy that nonsense,' she said. 'So now listen to me. I hate prisons, especially so the prison made of child needs. Can't you see the women pitiful in the cells of their children's needs? She would not go out because her child may need her breast; she would not brave the rains because her child may catch cold. I killed the child because I wanted to be free.'

'She is right,' said Duramani. 'The child is what the man uses to imprison the woman. To be free the woman must kill the child.'

'But the child was innocent,' the state prosecutor shouted.

'So was I,' replied Hawa. 'What I did was to redress the assault on my innocence.'
'What if the state redressed your assault on the child's innocence by sentencing you to death?' The state prosecutor asked.

'It's for nothing,' answered Duramani. 'The child will not know about the redress. So you are only doing it for yourself.'

'Who are you?' the judge asked. 'Who gave you permission to speak here?'

179

I replied, 'he is Duramani. He is a re-incarnation of a man who seeing the wastage wrought on his country by barbarians became a poetic indecision between faith and unfaith. He is an extension of an autobiographer, a starving migrant craving the pagan-skewed but divinely tolerated treaty of Hudaibiya; yea, a migrant from one-God/ess-Medina to multi-god/ess-filled-Mecca, lolling like a dog in the desert between these two cities of Ancient Hijaz. A poet is giving him the water of life. The poet has no bowl so he bales the water out of the well of the void with the shoes of his imagination. And the poet may yet go to heaven for that ingenious way of saving a creation. Your worship, the man who spoke without your permission is a fiction, a lie told by someone who is a lie told by someone who is lie. He is a base fluid big-banged onto the exploding expanse of nothingness. He does not catch his breath in this forced marathon where the winners' trophy is death and nothingness, and the losers' consolation prizes are also death and nothingness. Your worship, the breath itself is the nothingness blown into you by hesheit that was before our beginning. Ask your astronomers, summon them as expert witnesses, question them, ask them these questions: are the stars moving away from us, are the guiding lights speeding away in the expanding far layers of our universe? Your worship, they would answer yes, the universe is inflating, the heavens are moving away from us, going far away, so that we will not wipe our dirty hands on the clouds. Ah, your worship, so you don't remember that other African creation story about how in the beginning the sky was close by, but the cooks among us took to wiping the soot of their hands on it, dirtying it, so the sky moved away to prevent this dirtying of its purity. Your worship, are you still staring at the heavens darting away from us? When you catch your breath, it is nothingness, when you speed on, it is unto nothingness.'

'I must catch my breath,' said the judge. 'The case is adjourned.'

'You cannot catch it,' said Duramani. 'The breath has already slipped out through your lungs. The lungs cannot imprison life. Nothingness can't be locked away; our firmaments are nothingness-laden, death ever-drizzling down our skulls...'

'Well then,' the judge replied, 'we must build roofs against it.'

'Where do you stand whilst building a roof in this rain, is it not in the rain? Lo, you turn your back to it to build the roof...'

'But it can be done... '

'It's useless mate, roofs can't hold it out. It's a photon-rain, a wave nothing can stop, it's in your blood, brain, everywhere... what do you want to build the barricade against? It's not outside you; the rain is your memory, your story, it's you, the rain is you, you're death-drizzling, you're a dying... come on, acknowledge

181

it, embrace your dying, it's the way to happiness...'

'Tell me woman,' the judge asked, 'did your child embrace its dying?

'It embraced it,' Hawa replied, 'it did not fight to catch its breath.'

'That was a beautiful dying,' Duramani said.

Stories stories stories, the other time Sana wrote this poem about the woman, remember, whose son was murdered and had his thing cut off; remember, the woman that went to dispenser friend for medical attention. Well this was what Sana wrote:

We were sieving sunrise
With our eyes
Gathering fine rays
Into the calabash of our hope
When the revolutionaries
Riding the whirlwind of our discontent struck
Spewing our kola nuts
At our faces
Smashing the calabashes
Splashing the waters of our hospitality

They slave-marched us
The loot from our hearths
Pressing down our hearts

To the unwedded thorns of our earth

Lamin's face was bruised
Brambles pierced his back
But he dragged on
We dragged on
Sloughing off the tired
The weak, the babies
In the red slough
Of their bayoneted dying

Lamin's mother crawled alongside Lamin
Loving mother leaning against only son
With thighs the make of infant coffins
'Who's she to you?'
The rebel with eyes the colour of sunset yowled
'Mother,' 'son'
In unison each told who the other was

The rebel jumped like one whose loin
Was stung by giant ants
'Corrreeecct...' he cried,
'You have between you
What it takes
To complete the sacrifice
To the The-God/ess of our disposition.'

The rebels held mother rude
To strip her nude
And they said to her son 'Come on lad
Unto your mother

Spear her womb
And spare your tomb'

'No,' Lamin cried

The rebels dangled
To Lamin's mangy circumstance
Fresh skulls of slaughtered orders-breakers
And said 'Fulfill our dogness
Pee on your mother's bush and join us for lunch'

'No,' Lamin cried

They showed Lamin vistas of fame
Painted in his name
'This is no ordure
For the obscure
Come on, sniff
You are too young
To shun the dung
Too bright to be a blight
On the purity of our sin
Thrust man, that's the call of man'

'No,' Lamin cried 'I'll be decent to the grave'

'That you can't do'
The rebels yelled, 'You shan't die decently'
They forced Lamin's eyes open to their gang rape of his mother
And then plucked his eyes off
For the sin of beholding the scene of their sin

And cut off his thing
To hang on their flag
And left mother there
To die in the rot of her memories

I protested at the way Sana twisted the end of the story. 'You lying, Sana, Lamin's thing was cut and shoved into...'

'I know, but that's horrible, unprintable.'

'O yes! Go on! Censor truth with the alibi of un-printability; you worthless plagiarist!'

'Me, a plagiarist?'

'That 'no, no,' thing you put into Lamin's mouth; is it not from Soyinka's *Mandela's Earth*? Was that not the way Soyinka said Mandela bashed the Boer's offer to make him the mascot of their apartheid space ship? Or do you want to mount a defense of intertextuality to hide your crime?'

'Look, Momodu, sorry Adam, every storyteller is a criminal of some sort, a mutilator. But then they are mutilators for beauty's sake.'

'Like those who excise women.'

'Ah no, no, no, let us not go into that. What I mean is that every creative writer alters – after all,

185

recollection, in any guise, alters. Though, of course the artists turns their altering into an art. We, more than anyone else, assert the human instinct for alteration. Was it James Joyce who wrote that 'literature is the eternal assertion of the spirit of man?' Spirit? I prefer instinct. I prefer a whole lot... Literature is the eternal assertion of the alteration of manwoman or the eternal alteration of manwoman. Purpose? That we may understand manwoman. I got this idea from the Russian novelist Dostoyevsky. Remember when in his book, The Brother Karamazov, Ivan the The-God/ess-questioner said unto his brother Aloysha the trainee priest, 'If I should want to understand something I'd instantly alter the facts.'

When you alter, says Atwood the Canadian, the alteration becomes the reality.

But then sometimes, this could be dangerous to the person doing the alteration, so be careful. Ask Salman Rushdie. He was fatwaed for linking facts and fiction in ways that the mullahs say they should not be linked. He dared mix together century olds koshers of metaphors, he pushed the haram of piggy metaphors into the iftars of Ramadan; he fingered the brakes of the vehicles of metaphors, and the vehicle hurtle down the slopes towards the cliffs of anguish. Behold! there is the anguish of the void, the blind is removed from our eyes of faith, pain upon pain, but only them that have eyes of believers know. Pain in the eyes of believers, fatwa's the ointment.

186

'But were the piggy metaphors meant for Muslims? Were the vehicles for the transportation of believers?' asked Sana.

I replied, 'I don't know.

'Yes, tell us,' Hawa reiterated, obviously having in mind Sana's poem about destiny rotting away in the dunes of faithlessness, 'why should our destiny continue to be so smelly?'

'We're flesh, Hawa, sometimes the perfumes of the divine breathe can't mitigate the rotten smells of the flesh. Sometimes we smell the stench of sex in the fine wafts of profound love. Putrid, like Armah said of menstrual cloth.'

The alibi of menstruation; sex-craze men here hate that flow (in our area slang, 'flow' also means 'say,' 'talk,' 'speech'); women know that men hate menstrual flow, so they tell their overbearing men, 'look guy, I cannot make love, I'm menstruating,'

And the overbearing man will recoil in disgust as his thing shrivels in the Harmattan coming from the woman's flow.

'In the freezing Harmattan of the soul,' Cousin, sorry brother, sorry, Duramani or... flowed, 'one sometimes wishes hot hell (in our area slang 'hell' also means 'food') would come and heat you up a little.'

'Don't wish hell for yourself,' flowed the Preacher, 'hell is deeper than a whole day's imagining of depth.'

'What about heaven?'

'Oh, it is wider than a whole day's imagining of width. And in it are youths, perfect companions with luscious eyes. The Angel Gibril was showing Abu Ibrahim the marvels of paradise when suddenly the whole place brightens up.

'What is that'? flowed Abu Ibrahim.

'That is a youth of paradise opening hisher eyes. These perfect companions await those who exalt one another to truth and perseverance.'

'What's truth?' Hawa 'Pilated' me.

'I don't know,' I flowed

'Don't know?' She looked at me fiercely; the fury roasted me.

'Oh Hawa, 'I cried, 'your eyes are hot.'

'That's because they are bright; luminescence is hot. You've been scorched by the luminescence of a youth of paradise.'

Printed in the United States
By Bookmasters